# MILE MARKER 99

## JACK THOMAS REYNOLDS

ISBN: 978-1-955622-89-9

Published by

Fideli Publishing, Inc.
119 W. Morgan St.
Martinsville, IN 46151
www.FideliPublishing.com

*Dedicated to the memory of
Sherry and Ruth Reynolds,*

**Please don't ever forget the heroes:**

Those that are frightened but steadfast when others may run. Those that open their eyes to the perils of women, children and… men. To the heroes of every color; the rich or poor, every nationality, and every religious belief, from every continent. To those that won't stand by and let wrong prevail. To those that are willing to risk life and limb to help another human survive. To those that are deeply touched by the sadness and tears of another. To the ones that enter a burning building or jump into a rapidly flowing river. To mothers that risk their wellbeing for the life of her unborn. To the father that will lay down his life to protect his family from harm. To a soldier that will lay down his life for his village, his city and his country to keep the rights of freedom, equality and safety for all.

To those that dedicate their lives to heroic careers: Soldiers, doctors, Nurses, Teachers, Police officers, Firemen, Ambulance drivers and such. And lastly, to everyday people that are blessed with heroic compassion towards all of mankind.

And, oh yeah… to our friend… "The Creator."

Other books in this series include:

The Rape Nest
Oz One Of Ten
Tricked

# JASON/OZ

*Dear God, I'm worried about you; you've had to endure the sights of millions of us starved and tortured for our belief in you that will not be compromise.*

*It must have been painful to watch the cruelty of slavery and hatred that has taken place as a prominent way of life in our world.*

*I know you've had to watch over us for thousands of years. You've had to be so disappointed in our stubborn self-destructive disobedience...*

*You've had to watch as your creations turned their backs upon your teachings...*

*You've had to hold your rage against many works of evil...*

# CHAPTER ONE

# The Mile Marker

*"You shall not give any of your children
to devote them by fire to Moloch,
and so profane the name of your God"*

(Leviticus 18:21)

Sunday afternoon, 3:45pm. It was late in the month of November. Jason, a native of suburban Pittsburgh drove along the highway going east towards Breezewood at a much slower highway speed than most drivers that travel the often called 'The Pennsylvania Turnpike'. It is correctly named the 'Turnpike' because it is an ongoing speedway constantly turning through the mountains of Pennsylvania that rise and fall mostly through heavily forest areas without a city in sight for miles and miles.

Jason was in a world of his own. He was enjoying a brief moment away from his construction business and taking in the beauty of the fallen leaves of early November during this three-hour solitary drive. His preference would have been to have his side-kick Helen, riding along with him but her schedule would not allow for it. For about an hour and a half Jason had been repetitiously playing his favorite musical hit of the sixties by the singing group called The Temptationstans. The hit was titled "My Girl" and he repeatedly played the CD as loud as possible. He was bobbing his head and loudly singing along with the music like he did when he was a young twenty-five-year-old brother from the sixties.

He knew most of the words to the song and loudly sang or whistled twhen he couldn't quite recall the lyrics. There were brief moments that the CD was adjusting to the song or it had moved to the next song; during those moments his mind just kept on playing and singing the song so that it never stopped.

Everything was going fine with his one man travel party until strangely… out of the corner of his right eye he caught a very quick glimpse of a dark shadow-like thing or person moving parallel to him along the fringes of the trees just off of the highway. He drove along at a speed much too fast for any human to possibly run. That was strange in itself but he wrote it off as a figment of his sing-along imagination.

As he passed the next mile marker, he caught another glimpse of what this time definitely was a fast-moving human taking leaping strides through the brush and the trees and keeping pace alongside of Jason as he now drove more than seventy miles per hour. For a moment, he briefly turned down his music because he thought he could hear the crushing sounds of the trees and bush being trampled along the path. *Could it be stalking me?* he questioned himself. Jason kind of smiled and wrote it off as a scary but impossible thought.

Out of dumb curiosity, as he approached mile marker 94, he slowed the car a little and continued glancing into the forest every chance he got without spotting his run-a-long mirage. He now began to suspiciously look for the running shadow as if it may be following him along the highway just to jump into his car and tear him apart or… on a lighter note, it may have wanted to sing along with him and the Temptations as he drove.

After a boring couple of quick miles with no sightings of his imaginary leaping monster his attention was drawn to something new. "Now there's another weird happening I didn't expect to see," he said to himself while looking far ahead trying not to lose the beat to his head bobbing or the aspect of the road-side runner. Miles ahead there was an area that was seemingly glowing brightly like a humongous florescent bulb. Even in these still slightly daylight hours the brightness made it possible to see far up and into the mountainside in the same direction that he was traveling. This was all getting a little too exciting even for Jason.

He decided to play a game on his side of the highway runner. He sped up to eighty miles per hour knowing no one or nothing could keep up to this pace. And sure enough, his highway shadow was nowhere to be seen. Jason grinned to himself and said out loud, "Well I guess

I showed his ass not to mess with this Temptation wannabe highway speedster." But after slowing down a bit he drove a little further, and low and behold, there he was leaning against a mile marker post giving Jason a smile and a little wave as I flew by. In his rear-view mirror, he could see the devil turn in his direction and sprint back into the forest.

Within the next few minutes the weather conditions began to drastically change from a calm partly cloudy winter overcast into a sudden downfall of a continuously pouring of icy rain mixed with sleet but he didn't care. He was still headed to get one of his precious teams of grandkids that believed he was the alpha of the world. Their song didn't say "My Girl," their words were "My granddad," as if he was some sort of hero. This was causing him to smile ear to ear.

The windshield wipers were set at their fastest pace but they could not keep the dashboard glass clear enough to see for more than a split second at a time, yet… in that second, he continued seeing the lighted area ahead as if were flashing between the swipes of the wiper blades.

He was scheduled to meet one of his family members at 6:30 p.m. down in Hancock Maryland to pick up three of the grand's on their way back from Washington, D.C.

Something even more strange began to draw his attention. It was the stream of fast downhill flowing shallow whitewater moving against the flow of traffic in his direction just along the highway but down over an embankment. It hauntingly seemed to be beckoning him to take a closer look.

Most of the trees around this area were just beginning to become barren. Some of the leaves had fallen to the ground but the fall colors were still prevalent. The view was distorted by the windshield and bad weather but breathtakingly beautiful even on a day like this.

He mysteriously felt that he had not only seen this sight before but that he had actually walked into the very same water filled stream that was claiming its place as framing for this part of the highway at the moment. He felt as if this feeling was some sort of mysterious déjà vu.

He slowed the car even more while glancing down over the guardrail into the stream. He had an eerie sense that something strange was occurring or had occurred here or… somewhere near here that he had somehow previously been involved in; what it may have been, he was totally oblivious of at the moment. For some insane reason he glanced down, turned down the music all the way down and cautiously slowed enough to pull over just off of the highway for a better feeling or understanding of what was going on in his mind.

After a few seconds of seeing nothing unusual, not even the runner, he drove back onto the highway fast enough to merge into the oncoming traffic. After safely looking into his review mirror he quickly turned his attention back to the highway ahead to find that, right in front of him a huge man was standing in the center of the two lanes that were going east waving his hands in the air and beckoning him to stop.

Jason slammed on his brakes to avoid running him over. He instantly began to swerve uncontrollably… the car went off the road at an even faster pace, knocking down the highway marker sign and sending it through the passenger side of his windshield. This was Mile Marker 99, and it was suddenly embedded into his windshield.

His car slid and continued out of control crashing through a temporary wooden barrier placed by highway workers. In complete panicked he uncontrollably drove through a small construction area parking lot loaded with unavoidable piles of highway building materials.

Over a second barrier he went, crashing down a steep stone embedded embankment at a helplessly fast rate of speed. He was being tossed around inside his vehicle like something above was shaking and rattling his car like a ragdoll. Down and down he went until coming to an abrupt stop just inside the shoreline of the fast-moving creek. There he sat momentarily shaken and bruised with a little blood coming from his lower lip but other than that, he was uninjured.

He strenuously climbed over the center console pushing the mile marker sign out of his way. He unlatched the passenger side door handle and pushed with all of his might.

With the trucks and cars still roaring by up above him he quickly found himself standing knee high in the creek he had just been gazing into from above the embankment. Now he was literally standing in the middle of the fast-moving, ice caped white-water stream with the rain and sleet continuously pounding against his face and now soaked body. Without his knowing it, Jason was seemly very close to being in some sort of hypnotic state of mind. He glanced upward into the forest at the water's edge on the other side of the creek.

"Why am I so mesmerized by what I'm looking at instead of trying to get the hell out of here? I don't recall ever stopping here in my entire life and yet I'm being drawn by the curiosity that must have killed thousands of cats, not to even mention the running man shadow that is still lingering in the back of my mind," he said out-loud and very much to his own surprise.

In truth, Jason was acting on an unexplainable desire to now venture into this secluded forest area as if he had lost total control of his physical ability to not do so. He felt himself grunt inside like a beast that he was well aware of in his own recent pastimes when he was transitioning over into his other spiritual self as an angel known in his own world as Oz. "How did I end up here? There are no people in this area. No children, no predators, no life at all besides animals and the many standing and fallen trees."

Jason attempted to reason with himself that he could have been killed, yet… here he was. He began and continued to ascend up the mountain side at the other side of the slippery and soaking wet embankment and away from the freezing-edge of the creek against his own better judgment. He could not stop himself…

"What the hell am I doing? Have I gone totally mad?" Mr. extremely brave Jason from Pittsburgh, Pennsylvania was starting to become afraid of what was happening to him after nearly running over a man in the middle of the highway and crashing into the creek.

Over the last few years, he had experienced all kinds of unexplained semiconscious acts pertaining to his dream like obsession with the destruction of evil men. But… this all seemed to be totally different than anything that he could recall. Yet… he now found himself after wading across the icy cold, rapidly flowing water up to his knees… heading upward into the forest instead of somehow getting back up onto the highway.

He predictably and quickly lost his footing as he slipped upon the wet stone of the steep hillside and slid back down, splashing into the stream. He panicked, but using his balance he managed to catch himself before falling too deeply back into the fast-flowing water.

Though it was just the beginning of fall, the water was unbearably cold as he quickly scrambled to get back up onto his feet. With his chattering teeth and still spitting out what tasted like watery mud mixed with sand, he felt as if someone had just dowsed him with an unexpected bucket full of filthy ice water.

Again, he blurted out, "What the hell am I doing? God help me if I've totally lost my mind without hope. Please just get me out of this crazy shit. Oops, sorry about the cuss word, God," he apologized with a little impossible humor in mind.

Something inside of him at the moment seemed more powerful than even God and was driving him upward without a clue of how to turn it all around. It was an inward obsession that he was unaware of. It was in control and directing him as if he fully knew where he was headed and why he must be going there right at this moment of time.

As he ascended the bank, he began to inevitably and aggressively pick up his own pace as he got onto the more solid ground just above the other side of the creek. The song his mind was playing loud and clear was another Temptations hit, "The streets are dark and deserted, not a sound nor sign of life. Oh, how you long to hear your mother's voice," played in his mind. The song wouldn't stop, so he kept pushing on.

He thought for a moment that he saw something or someone off to his right seemingly watching him and doing its best to stay out of his sight. *Well here I go again with the imaginary road runner,"* he thought. *Am I becoming suicidal? Is this where my life has taken me because of the child protective indiscretions of my past? What is driving me in this conscious push to go into the darkness of this place that is surely filled with unknown dangers to say the least?*

This time his quick glance out into the darkness around him revealed without a doubt that he was not alone and that he was most definitely being watched and followed.

"I know you're out there!" he shouted. "You'd better hope you're wise enough to not get in my way, because I will hurt you and I don't even know who you are."

He briefly paused and turned around to see that the highway with all of its traffic was at such a distance that the sounds were unheard and the lights were just specks flickering between the shadowed trees.

It was getting darker by the minute, and though it had now become nearly pitch black his sight began to surprisingly adjust with visions of tree silhouettes ahead and all around him as he seemed to now be nearly moving at his own full running pace. Higher and higher he climbed into the forest like the Sasquatch or one of those unbelievable beings on a National Geographic's television show; yet he knew that every step he took, something in the shadows was still keeping pace with him.

"What kind of end for me will this be? How will my loved ones find me or where my body finally may lie?" asked Jason. *I don't know what made me foolishly leave my car or enter into this no-man's land in the first place. I've got 'a go back,* he thought.

He attempted to slow his pace and to turn around to head back downward but… his sub-conscience drive was still overwhelming and causing him to continue upward into the forest and away from where he had come. The obsession was beyond human belief.

"My God, what the hell is going on here? I'm being taken away against my will and I can't stop this madness."

Jason thought he heard a ghostly voice. It tingled his spine. He abruptly stopped running and placed his back against the nearest tree he could find. He cautiously slid down against the small tree and sat on the ground.

"Who is that?" Jason shouted, "What are you doing here? Speak up or I'll be forced to protect myself by kicking your ass." There was no response, just a rustling sound of movement in the bushes around him.

"I see you, fool. Dome out of there," he said in an attempt to get who or whatever it was to expose itself. Still… no response. And then came a voice out of the darkness of the forest, apparently spoken by a dark shadow of a being with only the whites of his eyes visible. He blinked his eyes in an evil way while looking directly at Jason.

*"I am here working on my subjects up ahead at the tree of life! The question is… what are you doing here angel Oz? And why are you disguised in the body of a faithless human?*

*Would you like to talk as a man or as the true you? Would you like to join us? We've been watching you. It seems that you haven't truly decided whether you want to be a servant of God or a satan of disobedient ways.*

*We can make you a leader of people if you wish. You would have as many children as you want, and can protect or sacrifice them to your own god or even yourself. You would be more powerful than all my understudies here on your God's earth. Come on, think about it, you and the likes of satan enjoying the pleasures of God's most beautiful women and children.*

*All these things and more can be yours this day. You and those that follow Yahweh have been one of the disruptions of my true way of choice and supremacy over humans and a more meaningful life for those under God's gifted word of human freedom of choice,"* said the easy to hear yet very frightening voice."

# CHAPTER TWO

# Victims of Oz

*And he defiled Topheth, which is in the valley of the
sons of Hinnom, that no one might burn his son or
his daughter as an offering to Moloch"*

(2 Kings 23:10)

"What? What did you say?" asked Jason, while trying to look around in every direction at the same time, still in search of the body of a visible being rather than just a voice.

A brief flash of winter storm lightning lit up the open area where he was now standing near center. The flash of light revealed one single huge oak tree just off to one side of a treeless burnt out circle of land that he had suddenly found himself standing right in the middle of.

Again, Jason asked. "Who is saying all these crazy things? Who is that? Okay… that's it, I'm leaving here now!"

Jason repeated, "Just as I came, hopefully without having to hurt somebody without knowing why or who." Jason stood and took a few slow cautious steps with his eyes wide open and everything clearly visible, even in the dark. He was feeling the presence of his and every other man's most denied lifetime enemy… that being, 'FEAR ITSELF'.

"*I said,*" the voice, boomed, roaring and thundering, "*what are you doing here, Oz. Where is your Chism? Have you come here to attempt to kill my servants again? I ask because no matter why you have come, you or she will not be leaving here as living humans.*"

After hearing that, Jason cautiously creped backwards with his back towards the giant oak tree and his eyes expressing fear while rolling around in his head in an attempt to see some crazy person up here in this wilderness beside himself. He was moving slowly with the obvious desire to get behind its huge tree trunk to protect himself from whoever belonged to the voice that had suddenly roared from out of nowhere.

As he slowly and cautiously backed closer towards the tree he stumbled over what seemed to be a metal ground anchor attached to a set of rusty metal chains running along the ground and going in each direction to circle the base of the tree.

"What the shit is this!" Jason mumbled, as he moved back away to see what might be attached and now pulling on the chains from behind the tree.

*"You know! You know what you have done,"* said the voice. *"These are three of your victims that are now my proteges that you have attempted to destroy along with the sacredness of this ground,"* the voice said still without any complete visual appearance. *"You cannot leave us now. We will return this place to a place of higher peace. There are many trees in this forest just as this one only without your chains of restraint. Here we may come and retrieve sacrificial subjects from those with the understanding of Moloch's laws, you now belong to us"* the voice said.

"This is all so crazy. I'm just a humble man of God, not a god of any sort. It must be an evil dream. I don't know what you're talking about but I am willing to leave right this moment. I have no victims to take from here or anywhere and I don't want to be any part of your world. These… whoever is hiding behind the tree, are not mine and I want nothing to do with this whole nightmare," Jason said as a warning that he was getting fed up with this whole mountainside encounter.

*"Then you too shall remain here with them and their undying spirits. Rise up!"* he shouted, *"and come forth to meet your new fellow comrade,"* It said to the so-called victims of Oz, while still remaining unseen and yet somehow gesturing to those hiding behind the giant oak.

As the three seemingly frightened evil men began to slightly stir and pull on the chains, Jason backed up a few more feet ready to fight for his life. The first victim peaked out and showed his hand and one half of his face, while blinking and snarling at Jason from one side of the dark shadow of the tree. His eyes appeared to be blood-shot red and sunken well into his skull. His face and the skin on his hand was shriveled and resembled a dried-up prune in color and texture, as if he had been there for many years.

Another victim appeared from the other side of the tree looking identical to the first but with a thicker body shape even though he too was also dehydrated. The third was apparently lying on the ground between a huge extruding root of the tree and the dirt beneath it. He had his skinny snake like body and his jet-black arms were tucked into the dirt, he too had a splitting facial image of the first two only just a little uglier with beady eyes and outward showing dried up blood and dirt between every tooth.

"Who are these people, or should I say, what the hell are they? Why are you accusing me of harming them? I don't believe I've ever laid eyes upon any of you before in all my life," Jason bravely said while starting to show some of his human anger. "Is this some sort of joke some-how thrown in with another one of my nightmares?"

"You-u d-do know w-who we are O- O-Oz." it said with a chilling stutter while stepping from behind the tree. "It w-was y-y-you that b-brought u-us here w-w-one at a time over the y- years p-p-p-passed. Y-you w-were jealous a-and e-envied o-o-our power and p-per-severance over th-those y-y-young ones g-g-given t-to us a-a-as gifts from M-Moloch," it said. Not only were they nearly naked, but there were old dirty shreds of clothing stuck to their skin in various places.

Around this one's wrist was a one-inch strip of bloody discolored and tattered cotton cloth that led from one hand to the other. The cloth was tide loosely to the next victim, yet long enough to reach around the oak tree to bind the two of them to the third that was attached to the right hand of the one on the left. It was connected to the chain lying on the ground and the same with the left hand of the one on the right which also led to the chain onto the anchor in front of Jason. They circled the tree while tied hand to hand.

Jason could not recall ever seeing any of them though there was something about their presence that seemed vaguely familiar. Jason was aware that there had been many times in his past that he seemed to unconsciously share his bodily tasked with someone or thing that came from with-in at times when he went into a dreamlike state of mind that seemingly always resulted in momentary blackout that coincided with many of his dreams about pleading children.

Suddenly, just like the many times in his past, he began to feel faint and his knees started to weaken. He often thought that as in the past, that it was due to the excitement and stress caused by those that stood before him in addition to the loud evil voice and the strange power that seemed to have brought him here against his will.

"Why is-you here, Oz?" asked one of the others with a southern draw to his voice. "You done brung another ta add to yo tally?" he asked.

Jason was trying his best to understand what was going on, but was quickly becoming so faint and incoherent that his knees began to completely buckle causing him to drop down onto them with both his fist still balled and still ready to fight.

His eyes began to roll up into his head. It was apparent that he was quickly losing consciousness. As he did so, all three victims went silent and began to creep cautiously and maneuver themselves into a striking distance. All eyes were now upon Jason. Now he had suddenly become their potential victim instead of them showing caution and fear.

The rain, snow and ice were now falling unmercifully and another flash and crack of winter lightning seemed to pause everything in its tracks. Jason was doing his damnedest to stay coherent, but he was losing the battle.

The three evil victims, still recalling the dominance and strength of their captor Oz, proceeded very slowly in fear as if they thought this may be some sort of trick to end even the miserable life they had come to know within this hell-like environment near Mile Marker 99.

One of the three slowly and sneakily reached out his hand and touched Jason's knee and then quickly withdrew it as if he had been burned by hot fire. Jason responded by jerking upward in an attempt to get back up onto his feet, but he just staggered a little and slumped back down onto his knees.

"Stay away from me!" He tried to scare them with a loud shout. "I'm leaving all of you in this evil place and don't try to stop me." His words and voice were weak and revealing that he was becoming defenseless due to something spiritual that was occurring in this so-called holy place. He fell back onto his side and quickly rolled over, back onto his knees in a fetal position. With all of his might he began to crawl away like a man with broken legs.

The three were beginning to realize that this wasn't a trick but that their enemy of eternity was truly losing his dominance and power. They began to gain their confidence and excitingly started pulling against each other by the chains trying to get lose. They became entangled while hurriedly trying to out-do one another to get Jason before one of the others did for the sake of killing him and perhaps set themselves free.

One of them managed to clamp his bony deteriorating hand around Jason's ankle. He began to drag him back within reach of the tree. After desperately clawing the ground in front of himself, Jason began to give up. While at first reaching, grabbing and pulling on Jason's clothing to drag him back to his death, the three victims suddenly slackened up on their grip and were overcome with a look of a total fear of their own upon their faces.

For a moment Jason weakly and faintly looked back at his evil child predators to see what they were looking at that was seemingly just above his own head that had caused them to suddenly have such a frightening expression of shock and fear… Jason found himself standing straight up but still unexplainably faint.

"I n-n-knew it w-was a tra-a-trap!" the stuttering victim named Chester screamed while attempting to quickly drag himself and the other two along with him and get back to the safety under and behind the mighty oak tree.

Jason had finally and completely lost consciousness as the three victims scramble in fear.

After a few short moments of stillness and silence, Jason gave off a very loud grunt, and an unexplainable few jerking motions. He had slowly risen to his feet seeming to be at least 2 feet taller than he was a few seconds ago. He slowly gazed all around and then upward with a sudden look and a growl as if he had found an instant burst of strength from above. And then… he gazed around as if this and every other place on earth was in his possession.

The victims were peaking at the spectacle from around behind the tree and slightly trembled causing their chains to rattle enough to draw Oz's attention. He had indeed transitioned from the man called Jason… into the ferocious angel named Oz.

# CHAPTER THREE

# Satan's Protégé's

*"I HAVE NO PLEASURE IN DEATH FOR THE WICKED, BUT THE WICKED TURN FROM HIS WAYS AND LIVE"* said GOD.

(Ezekiel 33:11)

Not so long ago these three victims, so to speak, that Jason/Oz were now encountering, were human murdering pedophiles that managed to get away with cold bloodedly murdering as sacrifices, their sex victims at every given opportunity. That is, until the spirit of Oz embarked upon an unsuspecting Pittsburgh man of substantial innocence named Jason Thomas. Somehow, Oz accidently discovered, while seeking a pedophile that had abused a four-year-old child from a heavenly place, that he himself could surge into Jason's body and change from spirit to flesh.

With determination, Oz decided that while he was in human form he could take it upon himself to rid the world of as many child molesting pedophiles as possible. This effort led to the restraining and bringing these three captives to this holy place to be held here forever with the inability to break free from this purgatory.

Oz did so to prevent the evil spirit within them from vacating their own dead human bodies and moving on and into another child predator's mind to continue the sacrifices of innocent children. In this holy place they could not separate themselves physically from the bodies that they possessed for the purpose of the evil acts that required another willing human. For evil to find a willing human it had only to wait until men or women found a way to become vulnerable during the use of drugs and alcohol or an over whelming spiritual lust to just blatantly violate the innocence instilled in the many neglected and unprotected children of God.

Oz had not so long ago made the decision to take it upon himself to take the life of a particular man that had raped and murdered his own biological four-year-old child while claiming to be under the influence of drugs and alcohol.

The man was sentenced by the courts of human justice to serve five years in prison after his plea of a 'need to be forgiven' because of his drug influenced mind at the time. And… He made the claim that he had found Jesus which has given him the ability to reject the evilness of the uncontrollable urge of pedophilia and even from being a self-serving murderer.

The court's inability to know that the man was possessed by an evil that was imbedded into his very soul and had used this human body to commit the same acts upon as many as fourteen other children without being charged by any court system. They did not seem to truly care what becomes of a poverty-stricken child's wellbeing and life.

Oz took it upon himself to take that man's life only to find that the man's body had become vacated. What Oz witnessed was that once the man's body was vacated by the spirit of evil and the child killer took his final breath at the hands of Oz, something transpired. Rather than Oz taking the life of the actual predator and the spirit, he had only taken the life of the physical body. The spirit possessing evil continued to move forward to impose its influence upon any open-minded man or woman that choose his or her moments of vulnerability to exist on behalf of a commonly worshipped god of thousands of years gone by. That god was Satin, Moloch and many other names that relied upon child sacrifice. All thriving on the rejected evil ways to oppose The Creator.

And now, after a substantial amount time, other spirits were attempting to trick Jason into eliminating one of the only places that could ultimately serve as a place to end their presence among people and their control of evil temptation. Oz's intervention had become a very unwanted factor for evil beings as well as the evils of mankind, especially since his unprecedented and somewhat divine attachment to Jason Thomas's human body.

Jason's body was needed to carry out Oz's own direct disobedience of The Creator by way of his own vengeance on behalf of the helpless children. Letting these three captive predators live was not an act of forgiveness, but instead, an act of unforgiving revenge.

So, there he stood… as strong as an angel could possibly be, utilizing an upstanding human body as his weapon. And then… out of the darkness came another voice.

*"You do know that what you are doing here is against the will of our creator, don't you Oz?"* This was a softer voice, one that Oz was familiar with. It was the voice of Chism, the arch angel of all earth-bound angels. *"You know that this holy and sacred ground has been contaminated by this evil that you have brought here unto it. Satan has cultivated it into his own disciple training ground against the will of the Almighty."*

"I know no such thing," responded Oz. "This breed of men and their evilness have no power but to remain contaminated by their own demons within. They are here in captivity to protect those that are vulnerable to the trickery and hate of our god's children and nothing more."

*"Then when and how will you let this all end. Evil things are prevalent where ever god's disobedience dwells. And, it is he, not us that will correct the abominations… not us!"* she repeated in a disciplinary way.

"Yes… Well maybe it is, that god has chosen me to initiate the start of their downfall for the sake of the children we love," Oz proudly said.

"But what of this man Jason that you have led into the womb of evil. He can be no match for powers of the disobedient predators that oppose even god himself. How will you keep the likes of him from unknowingly falling into their hands as he has on this day to Moloch's worshippers.

"Surely even you as Oz cannot always be of God and man in the same instance. You are just an angel not a god," she said. "Evil dwells in the heart and soul of every man that has been born on earth. The childish parable of 'hear, see and speak no evil' does not apply in the realism that evildoers have lurked in the word and the wisdom of our creator from the beginning of time and… through the self-creation of the man-made gods in the likeness of Moloch.

"There is no extent that self-serving gods wouldn't go to obtain the willingly sacrificed blood of innocent children. Especially those that have been sacrificed through fire and wars. The first born is ideally a part of the rituals of the word but any and all willing sacrifices contribute to the strength of those that stand against the creator of salvation. The sacrifices and worship enabled the likes of Moloch, a name meaning give, god, bull god/priest or giver to the bull of gods. They all do exist based upon a word that has given the word meaning 'choice' a possessive right to implement what are known as evil actions at all levels of human existence.

"Moloch (the Canaanite/Ammonite god) has many names among biblically-oriented humans. Some of those names include but are not limited to; Ba'al, (the fertility *god of the cult of the Hinnom valley), Moloch, Molech, Milcom, Malcam, Malik/king and many others that can all be translated to the word 'owner' or lord."*

Oz responded, "Jason himself is of sacred blood. It is he that has been willing to risk his own life for the sake of the children, either knowingly or unknowingly. In these days of rampant selfishness and personal evil acts, both Jason and I need to stand unopposed. Acknowledgement of wrongdoings have vacated the hearts of men.

"With Jason's faith alone and the help of God, it is he that can defeat the likes of self-claiming gods that are persuasive pedophile predators, as well as perhaps Moloch himself or even Lucifer. And… it is I who will stand by his side until our creator calls on us to cease. I cannot sit idlily by while children are suffering at the hands of the wicked.

"I will dispose of as many of them as I can while using the body of Jason. There must be a threat to men that conform to their own perverted sexual hungers and the selfish hungers of wayward gods, when it comes to the wellbeing and spirits of babies. There can be no greater violation than that of the abuse and murder of children.

"All that I'm asking for is the ability to stand up against this type of abomination while the creator is fulfilling his timing of biblical prophecy. With Jason, I can send the message of intolerance by way of death. The threat of death has no strength among undying spirits. Jason and I yearn to approach the body and soul of all those that attempt to disrupt happiness under the sun.

"And again… I will stand within him until the power of my instincts direct us all to answer to the final gathering horn of Gabriel," said Oz.

Chism paused with a look of concern while looking around and up to the midnight skies. *"Someone's eyes are upon us. I feel the presence of another angelic power among us as we speak. Are you here alone or have you brought another of us with you?"* asked Chisolm.

"No, I did not. I had no idea that I would be summoned here on this day through Jason," Oz responded.

"Yes, then we have an unwelcomed guest among us as we speak. Who are you? Who has entered this space?" she asked.

*"Yes, I am here,"* said the voice in an arrogant way, that had earlier spoke out to Jason. *"I am the real Oz of my own faith. I am here to set these victims of that imposter free to choose their own pattern of life,"* he said.

The three captives again cautiously peaked from hiding under the tree and the stutterer screamed out,

"Y-y-yes set us free we are s-s-sorry for what we may h-h-have done. W-we D-d-d don't deserve th-th-this kind of c-cruel punishment," it said.

Oz looked at Chism, knowing that she knew exactly who the imposter was but she was forbidden to respond to the claim of another obvious angel of a different sort. This angel had momentarily taken the visual form of Oz's human counterpart and was also disguised as none other than Jason himself.

Oz looked directly at who he knew was the real imposter and spoke forcefully and clearly, "None of these monsters will be leaving these grounds alive, including you, if you choose to interfere. There is no longer a place on earth or in the heavens for these kinds of child murderers. As long as I can lift my hands to keep them here and dead, this is where they belong until Judgment Day."

*"You are just one want–to-be warrior of your God. I could crush you and your human in a matter of seconds if I choose to. We are many and we have come with the blessings of those that recognize the gift of sacrifice as God himself has condoned,"* said the evil angelic imposter.

"The creator has given no such approval. He has said so in the holy book of Genesis and… it would give me great pleasure to rid the world of the likes of you, and your gods while I'm at it," said Oz.

*"Wait!"* said Chism, *"it is forbidden for any angel to harm another. Only the Creator can terminate the existence of an angelic being, even one as low as you, Satan. Yes… that is right… I know your name and all of the many other followers of you and the likes of Moloch. You are no adversary of God, you're just a figment of what it is like to cause the Maker to continue the promise of choice.*

*"If you can persuade evil to do evil, we cannot interfere. But… these are the seeds of the children that God himself has brought from the sacrificial fires of Moloch thousands of years gone by. And… these types of evil have been instrumental even to the present epidemic of pedophilia across the world,"* she said with the look of com-

passionate human concern and yet a recognition that he, Satan, is to be despised.

*"Then get from me, the both of you, and let me proceed with what is rightful according to the word of your God,"* said Satan.

"Wait!" said Oz in a rage. "This is much bigger than the releasing of these few due to the rights of choice. This is a violation of Jason's right to protect all God's children from evil and I'm not having it. Get from this holy holding ground or you shall lose your life here as well as theirs, despite the heavenly laws. There will be no choice to sacrifice anyone here on this day, or ever as I breath with Jason," said Oz, while preparing himself to stand in the way of both Satan and Moloch.

Satan looked directly at Chism and asked, *"Can he truly strike down a ward of your God? Is this possible for him to foolishly stand against what is written in the book of laws that are embedded into your spirits?"*

*"Is he right in his stance against God's word?"* Moloch asked.

Just then an unprecedented sense of peace came into the sacred area. The skyline above around the whole area suddenly seemed to glow. The trees circling the holy site began to slightly dance as a very pleasantly warm summer like dry breeze came out of nowhere.

"What is happening?" Oz asked Chism, while looking up into the night sky with a slight look of fear upon his face?

*"I don't know,"* responded Chism.

Oz, sensing that the presence of someone or thing mightier than all that even he has ever known had come among them. He along with Chism instinctively slowly dropped down upon their knees while never taking their eyes off of the moving nearby trees or the star lit skies above. The leaves remaining upon the trees all around them were softly rustling as if someone a hundred feet tall was slowly walking and brushing against them.

The evil victims seemed to know exactly what was happening as they began to panic and franticly attempt to dig down deeper into the ground behind and below the roots of the mighty oak tree. Moloch and Satan quickly without being noticed by Oz or Chism, sneakily moved into the shadows of the oak tree along with his hiding victims/servants.

"I'm getting the feeling that this may be a good time to pray," said Oz.

Without warning the three child killers stopped digging and hiding and came forward away from and in front of the tree. They stood side by side and shoulder to shoulder with their frightful faces looking upward into the night. They were transforming into the appearance of normal living men as if they suddenly had not been while living under the punishing conditions that they had endured.

Both Oz and Chism were still bowed and still motionlessly looking upward attempting to see what had come among them and what was healing the evil victims and... what are the victims seeing that was not apparent to neither of them. But all to no avail, for the two of them while suspecting that it was GOD Himself there was nothing insight here or above.

"Again, I ask you, what is going on?" Oz asked Chism, without a response of any kind. "What should we do? Should we get up and flee for our lives or pray like never before?

*"I said I do not know, but I don't believe we can run from who is among us at this moment,"* said Chism.

"Is it god?" asked Oz.

*"Please stop,"* said Chism. *"I have clearly said that I do not know."*

With-in seconds all three victims from behind the tree were straight forward. They had all taken on their normal human faces and their bodies were just as they were before Oz took their evil lives. The previously stuttering victim stepped up closer to Oz and began to speak clearly without his speech impediment.

"I am Chester Bowles," he clearly said in a voice of deception. "I was born in Pittsburgh, Pennsylvania in 1940. I was raised by my stepfather, Miller Bowles, until I was old enough to run away from home;"

"Who is he talking to?" asked Oz.

"At the age of 9 and before my step father had sexually abused me," continued the victim we now know as Chester, "almost daily until the day that I ran away and found refuge on a farm out in Washington County. There I sadly continued to be sexually molested by a farmer and his wife until I became close to being an adult.

"Eventually I found my way back into the city where I met a woman with three children. One month after I moved in with her I fell into the temptations and encouragement of Moloch. He rewarded my evilness and my own extreme unmatched lustful satisfaction from within with his praise. I had learned to become an abuser myself. One night I accidentally smothered my first victim while trying to keep him quiet. He was four years old."

"Now that's no lie," Oz commented.

Chester continued speaking to the midnight sky and said, "The four-year-old boy was the first of six that I showed no mercy to at the demand of Moloch, 'my god of child sacrifice'. I was overwhelmed by Moloch with what I thought was common and pleasing to him. And then… Oz showed up and declared my life to be hopeless and misguided. He physically attempted to take my life and handcuffed me and dragged me here to this place where I've remained ever since.

"I have no wish now but to be judged and mercifully taken out of this miserable cycle of deception. May God have mercy on my soul, if there can be such a thing within me," said the stutterer who now spoke clearly while visually starting to reveal the youthful body of Chester Bowles.

Oz and Chism remained speechless and had not uttered another word even to each other. They were feeling the aura of the Holy Spirit that was apparently present around them and listening without a choice, to the confessions of the three captives.

The second victim stood forth as Chester stepped back. With his head bowed in the way of submission he spoke sadly, "My name is Raymond. I also was forcibly brought here by Oz about 10 years ago and tied and cuffed to that tree next to Chester and Victor, who had been here for more than a couple of years before me.

"I had very little life in my body and yet no way to truly die. I too had been a wanting servant of Moloch who had engaged me into all sorts of the evil acts and perverted pleasures that child sacrifice could provide to him. I had constantly been engaged in temptation.

"I lived only to enjoy the experiences that were asked of me beyond the pleasures of the mutual relationships of women. I was blinded by the lust of his god-like ability to dominate me and the innocence of a child with his unstoppable heightened hunger to inflict pain rather than pleasure at every level. I too was under the control of evil and sadistic ways without remorse or any wish to change.

Now, I pray that I can be healed and forgiven as it is written. In the name of Jesus, I beg of you to have understanding and to forgive me. I too wish for mercy and the freedom to become a good man of God. I want to be cleansed of even the thought of doing harm to any child on earth. I want to live in the shadow and be a servant of our creator. Please take me from this evil place for a second chance with a life filled with peace, amen brother, and peace be with you." He too then stepped back as the third victim of Oz came forward.

"My name is Victor, Victor Smalls" he said with tears flowing down his cheeks, "I was the first to be brought here by Oz who had no right to judge any of us; more than fifteen years ago. Oz said that I was evil and that there was no hope or place on earth for my type of child sacrifices and molesting as long as he could lift his arms to strike me down."

As he spoke his wrinkled and blacken skin seemed to begin to clear even more. His appearance improved with each pleading word. "I tried to explain that at the young foolish age of twenty I had never known what it was like to experience a mother's love. I was always treated unwanted and differently by all my siblings. My stepfather seen me only as a bastard that was born to a vagabond off of a train that came through town and departed by the week's end. I was often under-fed and kept in the cellar, neglected while the others seemed to be happy and content.

"I, too, was a victim and knew no other way of life until the loving whispering voice of Moloch spoke within me. I was taught his ways and to obey his glorious ways. I took to him the submissive pleas of children under my attack. He demanded that I enable him to listen to the begging pleas. He demanded that I learn to relish the pleasures of dominance through a child's fear while a mother wasn't vigilant.

"I realize now that what I was doing was wrong and I'd like to repent and be forgiven for all of those evil and confusing thoughts implanted inside me while I was so blind and still under his influence. I am now so heavy hearted with-in because I now know how cruel those acts were.

"I pray for forgiveness. After all these many years of loneliness and abandonment I have truly changed my ways. Please forgive me and show me the right way, in the name of God I pray, Amen." With that as his final word, he too with a prideful smile humbly bowed his head and stepped back in line with Chester and Raymond.

All three of Oz's victims had stepped back into the shadow of the mighty oak tree that had stood so strongly above as it had in a protective way for many of the years gone by.

Both Oz and Chism were still mesmerized by the power that seemed to be hovering all around and above them. Oz looked up to the heavens and back down towards the pleading men and what Oz knew for sure that in his own mind that it was Satan that directed this lying testimony for sympathy and forgiveness.

Finally looking directly at them with angry eyes Oz spoke, "What is this that you are trying to do?" Oz asked his own captive victims. "None of you have left your ways or you would have simply walked away from this place by God's will alone. The chains that bind you are made of nothing but pieces of torn clothing. You assumed that they were the bloodied cloth from the Son of God's robe and that alone has bound you all to your deserved destiny.

"It is not I who has kept you here, it was your own wish to be here as a reward of Moloch for your loyalty and forbearance. Based upon your current change in appearance and your acclaimed pleas you are apparently being judged right here as we speak. I'm sure that the all-knowing God is quite aware of who and what you are. If He has pardoned your breaches, then there is nothing I can do.

"But… I must say this to you and yours, I will continue with a vengeance to remove all evils that are a threat to our children each and every opportunity that I get and regardless of your pleas or satan's trickery. You have not been punished near enough to satisfy the children of God that you so boldly tortured.

"Yes… I have judged you and I shall wait to be not only judged but rewarded by the Creator. I have no remorse for the souls I've taken or my judgment upon you here or anywhere between all of the heavens, earth or beyond.

"What I have bestowed upon all of you comes from my spirit within me as God-chosen. If I had my wish, none of you would ever be subjected to any of the temptations of Moloch, Molect, Lucifer, satan or any of the other names that the 'evil one' adopts in an attempt to be equal to our Creator and holy spirit through child sacrifice."

As Oz finished speaking, a whirlwind engulfed all three of the evil ones at once and lifted them six feet off the ground. The sound was horrendous as the three men loudly screamed and held tightly on to each other as they were dropped back down onto the ground after a few seconds. Moloch and such, seeing what had happen to his servants quickly turned and disappeared into the darkness with the three victims running somewhere near behind him. The Almighty's presence still lingered even though all of the victims and Satan had suddenly vanished into the night.

*"We have made the decision to let them free from this holy place and forbid you to bring them here again,"* said the voice of the new arrival.

"Are you god?" asked Oz.

*"No, I am Michael"*

*"And I am Gabriel,"* said another voice

"Why have you set them free?" asked Oz. "They are evil."

*"Yes, they are but, according to the word, they have repented and are entitled to forgiveness. They have been acting in evil ways but they are not filled with hate as much as they are filled with the evilness of those higher than satan. You must know that they shall be judged."*

"That has no meaning to me," Oz angrily said. "They are not humans that can be forgiven as such. They are satan's disciples that have no intentions but to destroy those that can be good and those that fear and despise wrong doings."

*"Then you should have taken their souls from existence, not brought them to this strangely sacred place. With the help of satan, they have rightfully been set free by using the word of god as a truth, though they obviously have no truth in them,"* said Michael.

*"You and Chism must come along with us to be re-indoctrinated as servants of the Holy Spirit and to assure us that you have not been contaminated by evil ways in opposition to what is good by definition. Now, both of you must come with us to be judge by your own peers,"* said Gabriel

"What of my servant in earthly form? How shall we go separate ways in light of satan's looming scorn?" asked Oz.

*"You must now leave him to stand on his own against his ungodly foes. He is of good blood and is just and strong as a favorite Son of our Creator. He will prevail based upon his own love of God and life. Let him be. He is well aware that his journey here would not be easy, that is why he was chosen for you… now we must go, as evil is still lurking nearby for revenge upon you,"* Michael said to Oz.

*"As for Jason, he must leave this place as a man just as he has come in,"* said Gabriel, *"and God will be with him."*

"May I have a choice of whether to go with you or to stay with Jason?" asked Oz.

*"No,"* answered Michael the Archangel, in earth's Judaism, Christianity, Islam and all Biblical faiths of earth, *"the choice to stay here now for the final fight against this evil foe is not yours alone. It has been an ongoing foe of ours and the Creator for thousands of years gone by and you are much too compassionate to stand against such a ruthless god as he."*

"Chism, please stand up for me and my dedication, strength and faith in God," pleaded Oz.

*"How many times must I tell you? I don't know what is going on in this level of life between heaven and God's earth,"* she responded. *"You're the one that has been taking all these things into your own hands with stubbornness and a snarling face, and now you have no idea of how to proceed from the wrath of what you believe is our Creator. I don't really understand you any more than I understand the meaning of this night here with you and satan. We're being taken up above to move ahead with the knowledge that evil has no hope or chance against what is right. As for you, Oz... I suggest you listen to your heart and spirit instead of your protective mind and... humble yourself before God with every step that you may take from here on out. For you to harbor a constant feeling of evil against those that sacrifice the lives of children is no different than the feeling of our Creator. He will bring an end to the hopes of all who have used mystic powers to overcome all that is good."*

"Is this ground still holy?" Asked Oz.

*"My goodness, you never stop, do you? I imagine that you will be returned here to go out into this world and continue standing up for your personal causes that you very well know you should have left to our Maker,"* she said with a frustrated and fading voice.

"Does this mean that I am doing the right thing for God and our children, by pursuing evil and helping to put an end to their sick quest?" asked Oz.

Chism sadly shook her head and followed the Arch Angels into the night, while whispering something unheard by Oz.

*"What am I to do with the likes of you and your earthly Jason?"*

"I'm depending on you, God," Oz silently prayed "to lead me not only out of this so called 'holy place' but also forward on to the next task on Your behalf for Your children."

# CHAPTER FOUR

# Oz's Judgment and, a Brief Look into Heaven

With the area again being caught up in a whirlwind of rain and snow Oz and Chism were escorted by the arch angels Michael and Gabriel over to the very surface of the mighty oak tree that had been standing before them all the while at this often-called holy place.

The two angels majestically bowed their heads towards Chism and Oz, they slowly turned around and beck-n them to follow as they walked into the tree as if it itself was a door to their destination. Both Oz and Chism slightly paused with the look of amazement upon both of their faces. The unsuspected liquid like movement of the tree that they had all been standing in front of, momentarily caught Oz and Chism totally off guard.

After a few seconds of hesitation Chism bowed her head a little and stepped into the tree surface headfirst just as they had done. Oz hesitated and then proceeded to reach out his hand and touch the bark of the tree with a surprising amount of doubt and nothing occurred for him. He raised his other hand and push on the tree bark as if to push it open like a common door; it did not budge.

Oz pushed harder to no avail. "Chism!" he shouted. "Where are you? Hello in there. What's going on? I can't believe this. I have stood outside of this tree more than a hundred times, to now find that it's not a tree but it's some sort of a doorway to whatever is on the other side." He pounded on the now solid tree trunk as if it would give way and let him enter like the others before him if he pounded and pushed hard enough.

After a few puzzling moments he walked back away from the tree while looking up into the now nasty weather and all around in silence trying to understand the meaning of what he momentarily thought was his being rejected. A brief spot of light appeared on the tree and the arch angel Gabriel stepped out and motioned Oz to come his direction. Oz cautiously moved forward.

"*Listen my brother,*" Gabriel said, *this place is holy. You cannot wear the body of the human and enter here. You must shed Jason's earthly form and enter in your own spirit form.*"

"Oh," Oz dumbfoundedly responded, "I see." Oz stood back for a moment, closed his eyes and mystically focused on his transition from Jason into his spiritual self.

In the meantime, Jason's body responded to its earthy call and came back alive in this site known to us as 'mile marker 99' this heavenly place that was being prepared for the coming of judgment day. For a few seconds Oz sadly turned and watched as Jason helplessly slumped and folded to the ground. Oz grudgingly turned around and walked into the tree just ahead of Gabriel.

Once inside and standing next to Chism he was suddenly distraught as he felt the inner soul of Jason reaching out to him. Being strong he turned facing the heavenly place he had entered, instantly seemingly to remember this heavenly place as being one of many Holy Heavens of his own past. It was vast inside with unending pearly white living marble looking walls as far as the eyes could see with bright blue skies above.

*"My God,"* said Oz to Chism after entering, *"this place has no possible way of being described. It doesn't look like a place that one can say is similar to any other place that can be imagined. You may have been somewhere a long time ago in your long gone past or even in a most memorable dream, but nothing is as mesmerizing as this. You can only imagine that maybe someone may have lived here in a story book as described in a child's fairytale. It is a sunny and bright fantasy land where everything is alive and filled with an abundance of illuminating energy. Living lights of all colors with living molecules that form everything and all that are here. Every particle is alive. It's breathtaking and*

*mesmerizing at the same time. It's a place of pure peace that has been hand crafted by our creator. It's as if god has embedded all that is pleasant into the eyes, minds, hearts and souls of all that have been privilege to envision. The spirit of what it is to be that which is truly good. Having choices have no place here, it is perfect and unchangeable. It is almost understandable why even evil thrives to reach this heaven at every turn just to rest from the weary task of being disobedient. I had forgotten what love and peace looks like", said Oz. "Who could possibly desire to disrupt what God has placed here before us?"*

Chism glanced at Oz and nodded her head in conformation. *"I can't imagine any possibility of bettering what is here within our sights,"* she said in response to Oz. *"There are no words. What more could the judges of what is beautiful ask for?*

*"I have heard that every speck of moving light here is a spirit of all those from every space throughout the gamut, that have transitioned from all life into their heavenly spirit form. These are the living souls of always, and every soul has been placed in a life of his or her or even its choice of what has been perceived by them on earth and all other places as heavenly expectations. All kindness becomes actual with unending acts of understanding and peace.*

*"Here in this place a teacher is a living instructor to all there is to know a teacher's dream is of what must be learned and yet has already been taught. A carpenter has built many mansions all equipped with pure love and satisfaction in this kingdom of god with the pleasure of his*

gifted hands and mind. Here is what every builder has always wanted to instinctively provide.

"A musician can play the perfect song to every listener's ear. A child is being with an abundance of love and all eyes aglow. Every woman is a perfect woman even in her own sight and a man can be no greater man than he is. He that wants to be an athlete finds his way to being nothing but the best, there is no second place, and even those that are last are the winners of each race.

"Those that choose evil will be evil without capability of harm or scorn. A mother can love motherhood and a farmer can grow abundantly all that is needed with pride. Faith becomes doubtless and wishes are just a matter of thoughts of things that are about to happen next. The excitement of danger and surprising changes are always harmlessly waiting around every corner.

"Jealousy becomes an understandable pleasure and hate becomes a fruitless cause of laughter. Questions are answered before they are asked and answer are just a race to be correct or even incorrect on their way to being corrected. Being pleased is to not be aware of a displeasures. Being out of harmony is an impossibility and satisfaction cannot be avoided. We become a light that can choose its own path to our own wishes and expectations.

"They have no hunger or thirst unless they choose to seek them as an adventure. No reason for hurt or pain. With or without fear, there can never be a dull moment."

"That all sounds frightening to me," said Oz. "Who will we oppose? What has become of foolish wars? Where will *we find enemies? The thought of everything going well is unheard of and beyond mankind's imagination. What will earth's humans have to say about the boredom of peace to come? I know it's what they pray for daily but how can they except such a change unless they somehow learn to have faith without the existence of fear.*

*"And… what of those that love disrupting God's laws for the sake of power among their peers that are engulfed in the pleasurable duration of failure?"* asked Oz.

*"Yes, I'm quite sure the creator has thought of all and every possibility that beings can conjure up. But isn't that why you are here? Can you live without a hate against those that have chosen to threaten the wellbeing of children on earth, or are you caught up in the ways of satan?* asked Chism.

*"Revenge would have no place in our hearts if the acts of satan were not a possible threat to those wishing to feel safe from harmful acts while supposedly being loved as children, especially those of innocent ages. I must admit that I will always have a problem closing my eyes to the despicable acts that I have been made aware of, especially since I've known of no remorse or willingness to cease Molech's subliminal suggestions to mankind on earth.*

*"I, too, must be taught to forgive without being suspicious of false acclaim or… those types of infractions must be recognized and removed to a place of permanent restraint,"* said Oz with a very unforgiving face that clearly projected a promise of retaliation. *"Satan on earth has been known to violate even the unborn. There have been times that he*

and his have performed despicable acts that have torn the very fiber of what god's word stands upon. I have yet to be able to comprehend what purpose evil serves. Nor have I been able to keep my peace while patiently waiting to see god become angered by the merciless acts of blatant evil."

"Then may God guide you and restrain your own hands of disobedience. Revenge is revenge and revenge belongs to the understanding creator of all, not you or Jason," Chism said.

"Then restraint must be turned into restraint for those that harm our children while tempting the lord in his will," said Oz. "I am sorry. I am pledged to come to their aid even if it means I must parish for it," responded Oz.

"So be it," said Chism, "and may God show you mercy as well."

And then came the voice of Gabriel, "oz, my brother, your judgement will be determined. When you are placed back upon human ground, you must make your own choice of how to resolve your hatred. Our prayers will be with you but you will not be given any advantage or protection from any of the heavens…

"For now, we are committed to giving choices and forgiveness to even those with ways we despise. We must do the deeds that He has commanded of us. With that, I must bid you farewell, for your anger is understood but is very disrupting to our assigned task of giving choices and even waywardness," stated Gabriel.

"We, as well as you, have learned that according to the Creator's word all are not harmless, but it must be *understood that the harmfulness of evil will submit to the righteous. The righteous must stand tall between what is recognized by God as evil and the pure at heart which can be vulnerable to the deception and trickery of satan. So… stand very tall my brother… so says the Word."*

"*Wait!*" shouted Oz, while standing at his tallest height. "*I am not speaking of the ways of heaven, I am speaking of those that are entrenched in the daily battles on earth and, on behalf of the lost, the blind, the helpless, the sick and all of those that have been left behind and confused just as the Son of God had encountered while here. The earth world is not heaven. Nothing there has gotten better, and nothing has truly changed.*

"*The deceivers have only gotten stronger, and hatred and jealousy, for whatever the reason, is dominating our pursuit of righteousness and hope of understanding. And, where there may be a flicker of hope and innocence they are being attacked by the reasoning that all is fair, even for the abuse and misdirection of gender and mind stability. Am I blind to think that they may be forgiven and become enlightened and protected from the misery of not understanding God?*

"*They are under the daily bombardment of the influence of supernatural negative temptations? What are the helplessly deceived to do? How can they empty their minds of self-godliness and fill it with righteous compassion for one another? What is 'choice' if the directions to choose from are all filled with persuasive subliminal sug-*

*gestions that lead to the death of sound and compassionate reasoning*

*I'm asking should I close my eyes while pretending that all is potentially well, and heaven-on-earth is on its way very soon? Should I doubt my faith and attempt to make an effort to expedite what I've been instinctively taught is right? Should I over step my capabilities and attempt to destroy the insurgence of evil among us? Should I be silent and pray? I have no power to, nor do I want the task of changing the world's indifference to God's plan.*

"*My bitterness has grown from humane and spiritual protective instinct while not understanding the wishes of our creator pertaining to my desired and impulsive reactions. I continuously hear the pleas of children and I am domed to recklessly stand in defense of the momentary and hopelessly frightened victims of unrighteous premonitions?*" asked Oz. "*Again, I ask, what else can I do?*"

Oz suddenly found himself dwelling again within the thoughts of men like Jason, Ben and Clayton awaiting their messages only from the voices of the slain children that they were blessed enough to hear. "If I stand alone in my task so be it, so will it be. I cannot help but to growl and attack like a lion. The sheep like instinct that is imbedded within me is as a sleeping heart until my own judgment day. Until that day I will be the predator not the prey. If I am called upon I shall stand, not to conquer but to protect with my life as I know it to be. Only the voice of the creator can be powerful enough to take away my determination to stand against earthly evil," said Oz, as he uncontrollably postured in a human state of pride and defiance.

Jason paused and patiently waited for an instructive voice hoping that it would be from the Creator. While listening for a response, the view of Jason's human activities intruded into Oz's mind from the forest below.

# CHAPTER FIVE

# Jason Awakens

Jason, the human factor, in the meantime had unknowingly knelt down onto his knees and fell to the ground painfully as his own spirit was separating from that of Oz's.

Oz was still gazing down to the tree of life and into the eyes and now limp body of Jason. Jason was now lying down at the foot of the tree with the eyes of three spirit like forms looking down upon him. The evil eyes of Moloch were also among those that were staring down at Jason but, he appeared to be staring directly upward into the spiritual faces of Oz and Gabriel.

"Don't worry about him," Moloch said, while pointing downward without looking and speaking of Jason: "he's ours now. Gather up all the small brush you can find. We're going roast him while burning the tree to hopefully destroy this gateway into all of their God's heavens above. No longer will this be known as a tree of life; this will be from here fourth known as a tree of death and sacrifice," said Moloch. "I just wish we had the innocence of a child to sacrifice with this scum of Oz from earth," he said.

"Surely," said one of the others; "you don't believe that this is the only spiritual passageway into the heavens."

"No, but it will send a message that what was here at this so-called 'tree of the children' is just another mere subject of our dominance right at the feet of their God. Including this tree being one of Oz's own vehicles of revenge against us and our right to child sacrifice."

The angels above must have sensed the notion of evil as the doorway of the tree turned from an open blurred vision to a solid surface, Moloch and his fellow gods hurried to set the passageway ablaze and destroy the way of hope and everything in-sight, to the ground.

The blaze was kindled and made ten times hotter than it could possibly be as they began to dance within the fire while feeding the flames and orchestrating sounds of their own music with the mere motions of rituals and praise of the evil one. The excitement being generated through their chants and dancing worship caused their spirits to become intoxicated enough to move mountains with their own faith. They were shouting and attempting to burn everything in sight.

Jason began to stir from unconsciousness and began to slowly crawl away unnoticed.

"Hurry!" Moloch screamed into the now blazing fire shouting, "Maybe the heat of our Satan will scorch the very robe of the son of their God himself,"

Up in heaven; the now aware Oz, was frantic but being restrained by the spiritual force of Gabriel.

Jason below, was finally able to get to his feet without being noticed and began to run out into the night as the heat from the blazing fire scorch at his back while the self-claiming gods stood inside the flames and dance to their own music of celebration.

Within minutes the flaming tree alone lit up whole forest with no other tree ablaze but it. The fire lit up the night in spite of the rain and sleet. Jason had no intentions of standing fast or continuing to even look back. He just ran as hard and as fast as his human body would allow him. Away from the burning tree and down the mountainside, in fear he went. He ran blindly as his own mind could hear the loud earth-shaking music of evil mysteriously playing a sound much like the rumbling of thunder around the tree in the night.

The music in Jason's mind began to play as he descended down the mountain side in total darkness. Song after song played loudly drowning out the sounds of evil that was being celebrated at the burning of the 'Tree of the Children'. The sounds of human love and excitement were fueling the energy he needed to flee into the night. His musical memories were filling his mind with the many pleasurable up-beat songs that he had come to know over the past years of his life.

In rhythm with the inhaling and exhaling of each breath that he took as ran was the music booming in Jason's mind was "Workin' My Way Back to You, Babe" by the Spinners. The words and music were powerful enough to keep Jason strong as it played loud and clear. It was like a music video or motion picture scene as he ran, filled with and matching the action of his own chase scene.

Every breath he took was in rhythm with of his own musical thoughts. Jason was now running instinctively and on pure faith as his eyes were mostly held tightly closed. Somehow, he knew that his enemies were not far behind with the intent of taking his life as Oz's comrade. Somehow, he knew his God was with him every step of the way.

As he moved swiftly the sounds were upbeat and fast enough to match his foot pace and the movements of all that was around him. As he slowed so did the rhythm and the beat of the mental music from his memory. It was as if his own effort to escape was in tune to keep him from sure death at the hands of the evil beings at the tree base.

Not realizing how tired his body was, he tripped again and fell to the ground. He rolled to momentary safety behind a cluster of jagged bushes. He lay there for a moment, even with all the danger around him, another song floated into his mind. The words led the way and his own voice sang along, almost to the point that he thought his rendition was better than that of the 1967 original.

The real voices were singing, "With these hands…" The song was so peaceful that it seemed to go on for hours, though it had been only a few seconds. Then the beat suddenly increased, just as he had to get up and get away. Now it was jump'n… Isaac Hayes' "Shaft" that got him scrambling and headed away from his pursuers toward the highway below.

He had run so long and hard that confusion and frustration had taken away his remaining sense of knowing who he was or where he had been and he fell to unconsciousness. When Jason awakened early the next morning, he found the ground covered with a freshly fallen layer of light snow. He was confused, but found himself right at the edge of the creek where he had started.

The bright and sunny morning was upon him much to his own surprise. What happen within the night was all a blur for reasons unknown to him. The winter morning had come upon him seemly instantly. Jason had awoken in the wet and the nearly frozen cloths he had arrived here in. Now with a very puzzled look upon his face he looked all around without any of his own recollect of what had went on here in what he thought had to be just one single night of some sort of mental confusion.

He finally began to remember crossing the stream ahead before his memory lapse. Up ahead he could finally see and now hear the noise made by cars and trucks going up and down the highway at Mile Marker 99. He thought that all he needed to do now was to somehow wade across the powerful ice-cold mountain rapid stream back from his mystery trek and on to the loved reality of his own family life.

Once he entered into the stream of icy water it didn't take long before he felt the strength of the stream pushing against his buckling knees as he got near to the center of the currents. The fast-moving water quickly and surprisingly rose up nearly to his underarms. Jason was a very strong man and was not about to give up on his effort to get back home.

Suddenly he felt as if both of his legs just below his knees were in the grasp of unexplainable huge hands. It felt as if someone was holding him so tightly that his strongest effort to step forward was impaired. The pressure from the current was pushing so powerfully at his back causing him to feel like an attempt was being made to sweep him off of his feet and down into the rapids to his doom.

*I've got to pick up my grandchildren and take them back home for the holiday. I can't believe that I've gotten myself into such a dangerous predicament. They are waiting and depending upon me*, he thought.

Suddenly he found himself fully engulfed below the surface of the stream. He was splashing hard while floating very fast within the current and now… truly fighting for air and against the water as well as the creek's rock bottom. He was again truly fighting for his life.

*Shit! I'm in trouble.* He was grabbing for anything and everything that came within reach around him; tree branches, rocks, mud and even floating pieces of paper, but the current was much too strong and prevented him from hanging on to anything.

Fatigue was starting to set in but he would not surrender. He spotted the frontend of a car that had apparently somehow ran into the stream and was wedged between the larger rocks. It was just above the surface of the rapids and he was getting closer to it by the seconds. *It's chance!* If he could maneuver himself close enough to reach and grab any part of it, he could get to the stony shore. He splashed and paddled desperately, it was no more than five feet from his reach and with the current he was getting closer quicker than he had imagined.

*What in the hell?* Something had now caught onto the leg of his pants as he got less than a foot or so from the protruding front of the car. He kicked and struggled to pull his one bound pant leg free to no avail.

"Oh, shit," he franticly whispered while intentionally going headfirst under water to pull himself back to what ever caught his pants. "Oh shit!" came again. It appeared to be the hand of a dead person with a full grip through a tear just at the end of the bottom seam. He desperately scrambled to undue his belt buckle as a last resort… It worked… he kicked and wiggled his lower body lose and out of his pants while simultaneously reaching the front part of the car that had just came into his grasp. He held on for dear life while spitting and briefly catching his breath.

Getting out, he began to climb onto the hood and roof of the car and then literally crawl across on its surface until mother-earth placed sound footing beneath him on the embankment. Suspiciously, as he looked back into the flowing water it seemed to be passive and quite harmless as it moved that section of its-self quickly down the stream.

In spite of all that had just happened Jason laid there early naked on the rocky shore just above the rear end of the car while the front end was still stuck in the moving shallows. He was looking up at God's blue sky while semiconsciously meditating about all the pleasant memories that life had bestowed upon him and his family.

Coincidently' the car that had saved him from the near death happen to be his own. *This was a very complicated day,* he thought. *How in the world did my car get this far into the stream instead of bent up on the banks of the creek where I left it?*

In the same few seconds of thought gathering, he wondered who or what had been so determined to prevent his survival and at the same time he wondered who or what refused to leave him by himself to perhaps die. Of course, he had a song named "Get Off My Mountain." He lay there, damn near dead, and sang it again and again, just trying to get back some of his strength…

He continued to sing "Get Off My Mountain" while lying there catching his breath. His mental music of peace was playing to the tune over and over until he heard a distant voice.

"Excuse me, sir. Are you all right?" The face of a small boy looked down upon Jason from far above. The boy had been taking a highway pee stop with his father, who was within hearing distance at the very top of the embankment.

"Dad? Dad! Hurry over here! There's a wet, naked man down over the hill!"

The dad came running to see for himself and excitedly began yelling down to Jason, "Are you all right? Hold on down there, sir. I'm calling for help,"

Seemingly within minutes Jason could hear the police and rescue sirens. "Hey down there, don't worry we'll have you out of there shortly," someone above him hollered, "Just hold on."

A young man from the rescue squad managed to climb down where Jason was now curled up and shivering. He hurriedly buckled Jason into a harness and yanked on it, signaling for them above to hoist him up.

"Were you alone in that car? Is there anyone else with you?"

"No," was Jason's response. "I'm by myself."

Once they got Jason to the top of the steep embankment they quickly wrapped his shivering body in a Pittsburgh Steelers blanket and led him to a waiting ambulance that was just pulling up.

"You're a lucky man." The rescue man said and asked Jason, "How did you manage to stay alive last night with the temperature near freezing all night while you were in that rapid flowing creek? God must have surely been with you. Do you know the other three men we found a mile up the highway? They were half naked too, but in very good condition considering how cold it was last night. You guys must be today's miracles. Are there any more of you in there?" he asked with a puzzled look on his face.

"No, I don't know anyone from around here. I was strangely, or I guess I can now say stupidly, curious about the area and decided to investigate by walking until I got lost. I think I did run into three strange looking men that appeared to have been in these woods for a long time, but after that, my memory draws a blank until I found myself in the middle of the creek fighting for my life. I don't know how my car got into the creek. I had left it on the side of the road after I accidently drove off of the highway near Mile Marker 99."

"Well, a couple of days ago there were calls from the Pittsburgh police department asking us to be on the lookout for your vehicle after you had failed to show up to meet your family down in Hancock Maryland. We drove all along here several times each night without noticing that the guardrail had been knocked out right here at this mile marker until now.

"As I said… we did find the three other seemly lost gentlemen. Different people answered their phone calls and came to the barracks to pick them up early this morning. They gave us no explanation as to why they were out here. The shift captain seemed to know of them and vouched for them as exotic campers and we sent them on their way. Do you think you need to go to the hospital or can you get someone to pick you up from the barracks?"

"Can I please use your cellphone to call my woman who lives about an hour and a half from here? I'm sure she is worried as well as the rest of my family," Jason said.

"Oh, sure," the officer said. "And we're going to need all of your relevant information to have your car towed up out the creek. The local towing company is called 'Mike's. I'll give you their number to take care of what needs to be done from this point."

Two hours later Helen arrived at the state police barracks to pick up Jason still wrapped in his Steelers blanket but alive and well with no reasonable account of what had actually happened the nights before.

When he came into her view she ran into his arms as If she hadn't seen him for years.

"I'm so glad and relieved to have you with me that I could say thank you to God every moment for the rest of my life," she said, while holding him as close as she could. "Please don't do this again. Everyone that knows you experienced a feeling that we would never see you again. It was like some sort of spiritual face-book message that you were in trouble somewhere without hope.

"We all drove back and forth from Pittsburgh to Hancock in different cars while calling every police barracks from here to there, just hoping and praying, trying to find some clue as to where you could be for the last two days. Your children were frantic and all we could do was pray, and it worked. Thank God! Oh, thank You, God. Those were two of the worst days of my life."

Jason pulled back away from Helen's grasp from the waist up in surprise, "Two days! I thought I was only gone for a few hours... You know what... never mind what I thought. Please just get me home. I'm tired, I'm cold and I'm completely confused, and I'm not very far from calling myself completely crazy. I'll explain the best that I can when we get back home." Jason said.

In the meantime, Chester, Raymond and Victor, had gone their own evil separate ways and off to being welcomed back to their own domains after their long disappearance from those that they had known and abused. They all were expected by Oz to not waste much time finding their comfort level among unsuspecting families with children. Just how comfortable they would be with Oz or others like him constantly on the lookout for them, remained to be seen.

After being back home with Helen for a few weeks, It wasn't long before Jason began to hear voices in his dreams again like he had long before, and it wasn't long before his dreams of Oz hunting down the child molesters started him to yearn to answer the children's cries for vengeance on his own.

# CHAPTER SIX

# A Hated Victim

## *Victor Smalls*

January 10th, 2019, it was a cold night in the East Hills of Pittsburgh: At 3 a.m., after more than a month of attempting to fill Helen in on exactly what had happened that night at mile marker 99, Helen awoke to find that Jason was missing from her side.

"Oh no, not again. Please God let him be down stairs. Jason! Jason!" she shouted, there was no answer. She rushed down the stairwell hoping that he just didn't hear her yelling. He wasn't there. She sat down at the bottom of the steps in frustration. She had hoped that these night-time adventures were in their past after the Mile Marker 99 incident.

She noticed that his coat and boots were gone. After further investigation she also seen that his 44-caliber weapon and holster were also missing from their hanging place in his closet. His cell phone was sitting on the night stand at his side of the bed and... there was a scribbled note that read 'Victor Smalls, Frick Park' written on a torn piece of magazine. Frick Park was a local park where most people came to walk their pets or just to exorcise on the tennis courts or… the city had provided a few ball fields and other sport attractions. Her first inclination was to immediately get dressed and drive to the park to find him.

Without further thought she got up and began to dress to go out into the night in search of her man. She gave quick thought to the cold temperature outside, the darkness of the night and the thought of lurking animals. She shuttered a bit and decided it would all be worth the risk.

After the fifteen-minute drive she arrived at the park's upper parking lot and found Jason's car and another vehicle parked side by side. It was an older model white ford. She observed what she thought was exhaust smoke coming from the tail pipes of both cars apparently, they were both running idly. If she hadn't known and trusted her man she would have thought that this was a lover's rendezvous.

She slowly drove by the lot without drawing any attention to herself or the car, she parked across the street more than a half block away where she could observe both vehicles.

In the meantime, Jason sat there in the passenger side seat of Victor's car.

"Well Mr. Victor as you well know I've been stocking you for more than a month due to my own nightmares and of course the night flashes about the incident at mile marker 99, that I really didn't have the privilege of participating in. I've been in search of you based upon your intentions as a pedophile out among children again. I can't tell you how or why, but I've been almost hypnotically seeking you and someone named Raymond and of course your friend and Oz's, Mr. Chester Bowles. Today's phone call from you was a surprise given the fact that you seem to know that Mr. Oz and I are somehow one of the same and that I want to do right by all of you while he seeks to harm all of you rather than anything good."

"Yeah, I know, but I'm tired of looking over my shoulder for Oz. I think it's time for me to be left alone with the human side of my endeavors. I can't do it with you or Oz constantly ruining my chances of pursuing my own happiness," he said while building his confidence to speak with more of a demanding authority.

"I know dammed well that you and Oz are one of the same. And I think I've got a much better chance with you than Oz's unforgiving intentions of killing me and my spirit without an attempt to understand my plea. My whole life has been filled with nothing but the haunting desire to bring out the fear and childhood anxiety that gives me the power and satisfaction of my calling.

"You and yours may call it a sickness but we know for sure that it's an unending, uncontrollable and unexplainable lust that is instilled within us by our god to deliver the souls of sacrificed innocence children. None of us in existence need a reason or rhyme. All we need is just an opportunity and the rest is done by our instinctive overwhelming pleasurable lust. No one seems to really care but, the joy of evil is our return for Satin's blessings beyond all the sexual moments of life," Victor boldly said to Jason.

"Well I'm here with you whether you want to call me Oz or by my name on behalf of my own Creator and the spirits of all the helpless children you and yours have disrupted. I stand against what my maker has called the world's 'most despicable act. Listen…" said Jason filled with the shrewdness of Oz. "Our God also states that suicide is an unforgivable sin. Why don't you and yours join together and achieve a common thread that takes your own lives to the ultimate goal of evil.

"And you, Raymond and Chester can be one of first to award Satin with the satisfaction of a much higher violation of God's demands. It is said that suicide is much like the satin's thrill of a thousand orgasms at once," Jason knowingly and fictitiously said.

"You must know by now that whatever thrill you get from raping a child Imagine what it will be like at a thousand times greater. Come on, try it. I'll help you. You will become as great or greater than Satin himself hopefully for eternity," Jason said to encourage Victor. He could see that Victor's own aspirations of being as his own god were tempting his inner desires. "What would you have to lose? Surely Satin did not say that there is a greater gift to him. And this gift from you would be a thousand times greater. All the world of Satan will be grateful to this new direction that you and you alone can boldly declared. This will be your choice. The choice that God has often spoken of in the human bible."

"How will I be able to do it?" Victor asked. "I know that it is forbidden by many of the gods. I'm not so sure you are speaking the truth."

"With such a powerful pleasure as this, I will assist you and justifiably remain jealous of your journey into your own bliss. Just sit here and enjoy the ride to utopia."

"But where are my loving children? How will they learn the glory of being sacrificed to my king of kings?"

"Don't worry the children will be delivered to you just as they are to Satin and Molect during their rituals of burnt offering for the forgiveness of earthly sins against the commands of God The Creator. Trust me, I'm telling the truth. To take your own life before the life of one of God's children will be rewarding and glorious as a follower of Satin."

"I don't know…" hesitated Victor, "I've not been told of a pleasure regarded more highly than the selfish infliction of man's control over a frightened innocent child of God."

"I deceive you not. Satin has gone too far extents to cause evil within the hearts of men, and maybe he is aware of something that your child hunger has not revealed. Maybe this is the pleasure that he hides from you beyond your quest to deliver sacrificed souls for him to lavish upon. Maybe in haste to become as God he has left a void for you to singlehandedly fill with your own discovery of eternity and god-like superiority.

"Please just let me help you on your way to being a god not only on earth but among the gods of eternity." Jason got out of the car and grabbed a piece of flexible plastic hose from a cable blocking off the 'do not enter' sign at the rear of the parking lot. He proceeded to stuff it around the rear exhaust pipe and into the partially rolled down rear window of the car.

He got back into the car with Victor as Victor had dug out some child porno pictures he had been carrying in his glove compartment and was looking at them under the dome light, "These are some of my very own little lovers of my past. Would you like to take a look?"

"No thank you," answered Jason. "You just enjoy the ride please. And… take a little nap while you wait to lead the way for all that I can get to follow in your foot-steps to worship you… please."

After a few moments, Helen watched as Jason got out of the passenger seat of the white car and walked around and opened up the rear driver's side. He opened the door, reached in for a few seconds. He then got back out and slammed the door. He, got back into to his own vehicle and calmly drove off.

She ducked down a little as he passed by her and her car without noticing it being parked between two others. She pulled out after he passed and hurriedly drove a different direction home hoping to arrive before he got there.

When she pulled into her own parking lot she noticed that he had yet to get there. She had quickly walked to the front door of her apartment when his car pulled into the lot. She fumbled with the keys before realizing that she was not going to make it in without being seen.

She turned around as he was walking up the walkway and approached him, saying, "I was just coming out to find you honey. I was worried that you had left your phone and I was hoping you would be safely over your sister's house. With all that has gone on recently I guess we are all still a little on edge," she said while pulling herself against him.

"I'm all right," he answered. "Some unfinished business was bothering me. I'm sorry. I didn't want to worry you so I went on my own to see if I could resolve it."

"Jason… are you involve with another woman?" she calmly asked while knowing that wasn't the fact. "If so, please be man enough to enlighten me. I don't know how I will respond but I do know that I am woman enough to deal with whatever comes our way. And… I should be entitled to at least a fair chance to compete for the love of my chosen mate against anyone or thing under the sun."

"I understand why you may be suspect of my behavior. Let's get into the house where it's warm so I can attempt to explain why I think I have been acting so radical." They entered and removed their coats and boots. Jason led her up into their bed room where he placed his weapon back where it belonged.

"Why did you need to take your gun with you? Is someone threatening you Jason. Because if they are we need to involve detective Ben or detective Clayton or your other policemen friends. I'm very afraid of all the things that you've found yourself in the middle of over the last couple of years.

"I know that the things we've gone through together have been unbelievable and I appreciate you as a man of distinction and, of course, a man of God but I want so much to take us into the normal life of love and happiness before we chose to do God's work or anything else, hopefully together."

"If you think that I'm capable, as a man, of breathing without you in my life, then you too have become disorient with all of the un-understandable impossibilities that have worked their way into my purpose of life. The answer is, no there is no other woman.

"I'm not privileged enough to understand God's wishes, so it seems I live on with a heaven-sent vindicator within my mind and soul. It seems that as imperfect as I am, I've been chosen as a tool that speaks with judgment of those that are harmful to the true word of God and his passion for the innocence that is preserved within children.

"At times I am as confused as to what does often possess me that I just simply yield myself as if I'm in a trance. Hopefully, I pray that I'm always in the right hands. This night's escapade is clearer to me than most of those of my past," a tearful eyed Jason confessed to Helen that, "On this night, I believe, that I alone, as Jason, have assisted a man in taking f his own life. I don't clearly know the details but I know that I wished him to leave this place and answer to his maker, even though I'm not quite sure why.

"I went there to rescue him from his own insanity and ended up assisting him. My demeanor was cold, unforgiving and heartless as if I myself had judged him and administered his punishment with pleasure and also the applause from his many abused youthful accusers"

Helen sat motionless and hesitated to respond. And after a few seconds of thought she abruptly stood and bravely said, "I don't care! I have faith that you are somehow directed by what is good. I am the woman that has been blessed and inspired by you in every way to follow your unselfish premonitions and to do what you are instilled to do.

"You have been an inspiration to those, including me, that have taken the time to know your heartfelt love for God's wishes whether you see them as being right or wrong. When all the dust of evil clears I'm sure you and many others like you will be bowed down beside our creator. Thank you, Jason for standing strong for the righteous and people like me that wish only to live in safety and peace."

"Wow, that was a little strong and certainly above me but I do hope to be on the good side if and when needed," responded Jason.

"Can I read you a prayer that I wrote since the mile marker 99 incident," ask Jason. "I believe I kind of mentally collaborated with the spirit of Oz and wrote down my concerns for our creator without even knowing how I can have the audacity to think that the all mighty may have the same inner feelings that we are burdened with as compassionate men and women. None the less, this was my prayer/poem."

God… this prayer is for you:

*There cannot be anything in existence that is under a more compassionately challenged task than you must be.*

*There is no end to our lack of faith nor our turned ear*

*It seems that we can only be loyal to ourselves and the frivolous out stretched desires with-in us*

*Given all that we have been gifted with; our shallow minds can only wish for more and more*

*Having love for our creator is seemingly much too strenuous and time consuming; we can only yearn and dream of being loved by all*

*Our view of a perfection can only be built around our own selfish observations*

*To the majority of us, you do not even truly exist… yet we cry out for all that you are willing to give*

*In recent days I've heard many prayers that start with the quote "Dear father God". So…. I would like to begin a poem with "Dear Father God'. Not to you but for you.*

*Dear God, I'm worried about you; you've had to endure the sights of millions of us starved and tortured for our belief in you that will not be compromise.*

*It must have been painful to watch the cruelty of slavery and hatred that has taken place as a prominent way of life in our world.*

*I know you've had to watch over us for thousands of years. You've had to be so disappointed in our stubborn self-destructive disobedience…*

*You've had to watch as your creations turned their backs on your teachings…*

*You've had to hold your rage against many works of evil…*

*Many have died in your name. It must have been painful to watch*

*I can't imagine what it must feel like to see children tortured or abused. What is equal to our tears, I'm sure have fallen upon your heart a trillion times.*

*Against your will hate has obviously grown somewhere inside of us and has disguised itself as compassion.*

*Please don't give up.*

*Take a long deep breath... then find enough faith within yourself to ease your own pain. Our innocent children love and understand you and will always be here to give you the strength that you must need to carry on as the all-knowing Creator of mankind.*

*Call upon us when you believe we may be ready to give something back.*

*If there is one above you I pray that She will show you the way. I cannot equate to how you must feel in your moments of loneliness that may make its way to your soul. Try and feel better. We will somehow (with your help) learn to make life easier for you...*

*Truly I say unto you Amen'*

***

The next day, the Pittsburgh morning paper read:

The body of a man identified as Victor Smalls was found early this morning at Frick Park in an idly running car. He appeared to have committed suicide by asphyxiation. Police are investigating for foul play.

"You know I think I've heard that name but I can't place it with a face," said Jason.

The man was later confirmed as a suicide victim. Mr. Victor Smalls has no known family members.

# CHAPTER SEVEN

# Raymond the Addict

## WEEKS LATER

Jason had heard on the streets of East Hills that Victor Small's hanging buddy named Raymond, another man Jason had been looking for, was no more than a heroin addict that lived in the basement of a vacant house located over in nearby Wilkinsburg with a couple of homeless families.

Jason took a day off and parked his car off of the main street and walked along a side street known for its number of vacant homes and drug addicts. He ran into a couple of street pan-handlers and played a hunch.

"Hey" he said as he walked up to them, "I'm looking for Raymond. It was dark the last time I was up here and I don't know which of these places he lives in. If you happen to see him, can you tell him I've got some really good shit, but I'll be leaving town in couple of days…"

"Yeah, we know 'im. I'll go get 'im right now. You just wait right here. Can you give us a little hit if we get 'im for ya? You ain't no roller, are ya?" (A roller was a name given to undercover police officers way back in the sixties.)

"No, of course not. Would I be bringing him some China White if I was a roller?" Jason quickly reasoned in his mind that Raymond might recognize his face and be spooked away, so he wrote down his number and gave it to the panhandlers along with a five-dollar bill and said, "Here, give him my number. Tell him to call me as soon as he can."

Jason stood and watched as the two men went up to an empty brick house on the left, slid through the hedges and down into the basement stairwell. "Gotcha" he said to himself. He turned and walked away, smiling without looking back. He knew he had located another rapist. Now all he had to do was devise a way to get to him.

The next day around noon, sure enough, Jason received a phone call from Raymond on a private number.

"Yeah, this is Ray," he said with a slurred, rather lazy sounding voice. "I'm calling bout the China. Who this? Where I know you from?"

Jason quickly responded, "This is Jay. You may not remember me. I met you at a cookout gig a couple of years ago. You were with a friend of mine and we got buzzed together. I was coming through the Burg and have some good shit. I thought I could pay you back for the free hits you gave me back then. What've you been up to?"

"I ain't up to nothin'. I'm just chillin' and layin' back waitin' fo my ship to come in. When kin I get it man? I could a good hit right about now. When can we hook up?" asked Raymond.

"I'm gon'na be over that way tonight bout 10:30. You have everything we need to get a little treat?" Jason asked. "Can I trust who gon'na be there? I'd rather it be just you and me. I'll leave you with enough for any of your company to hit on when I head out," Jason said. "You know, 'cause I don't know the others and I'd feel safer."

"Yeah… okay, we don't have no lights but we got candles and some hot used needles or you can bring your own. Don't matter to me. Ain't nobody gonna mess wit you here, dis is my turf. But I'll make 'em stay out 'til we get done," Raymond said.

"Hey, thanks man. I'll see you then. Want me to bring a little fent to add to the China? I got some shit that will knock down an elephant if you think you can stand the pain," Jason said.

"Shit yeah, bring it on, brother. I need it right through here," Raymond answered.

Jason was set. Now all he had to do was quickly find out where to get some drugs for his target. He was starting to feel concerned but still determined. He had heard that finding drugs in our black poverty-stricken areas have never been a problem but Jason had never actually been in the drug arena. He sought out to find a nearby drug dealer, they seemed to be everywhere these days, so it was just a matter of asking anyone on the streets. He invested in $200 worth of heroin and another illegal substance called black beauty that he'd never heard of. He'd heard that heroin users were adding it to their injections for a stronger buzz in an attempt to reach that often-sought-after final height of utopia. He purchased a needle for himself to fill with saline.

His plan was to join the get high party and pretend to outdo Raymond. His hope was this would cause Raymond to overdose. It wasn't as good as suicide but it was better than outright killing him.

Jason was ready. He headed for the South street address just before dark with the intentions of feeding Raymond all that he needed to get where stone junkies go to reach their goal of the ultimate high. However, Jason did not have the cold-blooded revenge seeking spirit that Oz seemed to have when it came to knowing who and what to forgive.

On his way to his destination he stopped more than once in an attempt to back out of his plot and let God or the law take care of this well-known violent pedophile. Each time he paused his mind took him back to the many children that he knew that this man had violently raped and more than once had taken a life.

He was so torn that he placed himself in the mindset that, if this guy Raymond showed any sign of remorse, he would back off and leave and then continue to pursue Chester and the devil that Jason knew was being carried with-in him.

Jason knew that he alone was never able to heartlessly kill without Oz or being inspired by the many violated babies. So, there he was desperately trying to know that he was an answer to a call of God by being His tool that he had often wished to be. He also knew that Oz's vengeance was unavoidable had he failed to act. And whether it was Oz at work for God and the children or he himself, he would likely be held responsible in the courts of law and maybe even in the courts of heaven. So… there he was, less than two blocks from his destination and getting a little bit of cold feet.

Now… right in front of Jason, there stood the five vacant homes. They all had broken out windows and the one he sought was right in the middle with the high hedges sitting there just waiting for his arrival. He paused again for a moment and took a very deep breath. He was truly ready. He took his little packet and tucked it under his arm. He patted his weapon he had named Betti-Lou that was under his shirt at his side and boldly stepped from his car.

He then quickly headed for the open space between the hedges and almost ran down to the entry at the basement level where Raymond lived. The door was closed and locked. Jason cautiously knocked on the door. He was still concerned that Raymond may recognize him as Oz. He had on sunglasses and attempted to wear a facial expression that even a friend wouldn't recognize.

The latch on the door was turned from the inside. A face appeared through the slight opening.

"Come on in my palace man I've been waitin' for ya. I couldn't get everybody out but it is what it is. The rest of deeze is my family. Joe over dare in da-chair has been stoned for da last three days. He don't know or care if we exist. Dat's my bitch on da couch, she just came in wit her two kids just to get her high on. I'll put dem kids in the back, day gonna be my belly warmers later, if you know what I mean. You don't got'ta worry 'bout dem.

"Da little girl is 'bout six and I think he's bout eight. They both mine," Raymond boasted with a disgusting smile. "Get on back dare wit yo kids, woman. Me and Dr. Jay or Mr. Jay… whatever… we got business to handle. You can get ready for me after I'm done out here. Get on now, you heard me." He pushed her hard from the behind and smacked her on the ass 'cause she was movin' too slow.

"Now," he said while looking right into Jason's face without a clue of who he was, "let's see what ya got there, big nigga."

They both sat across from each other at a small make-shift table with a small lit candle in the middle. Jason opened his packet and rolled it out in front of Raymond with four syringes already filled with dope.

"This one is 'Boy' mixed with what I call my night surprise," he said, while grabbing the one he made for himself and rolling up his sleeve as if he knew what he was doing. He began plucking on his veins like he had seen junkies do in the movies.

After seeing Jason start it up, Raymond anxiously did the same as he waited for Jason to shoot up first.

"Is all dis shit mine?" Raymond asked with a boyish look of excitement.

"Yeah… it's all yours, brother. Plus, I got some shit that will blow your mind if you're man enough to take it. I've already loaded my hit with it. If you got the balls, take the other needle and enjoy the ride to heaven…" Jason said, then whispered, "or hell," under his breath.

"You aint said nothin'. Gimme da shit an let me show you what real men kin do. I wants ta take both of these at da same time" he said as he snatched the remaining drugs from Jason's hands.

"If you like it and survive the ride, I'll get you all you want 'til you find your dream," Jason said with his own devious smile. "For you I even got some China Black, and to not be prejudiced, I've got some spiced-up China White too," Jason said in a street joking way. "That shit will get you high and give you the biggest hard-on you ever seen … except for mine, of course." Jason joked.

Before Raymond had the chance to use any of the drugs Jason had handed him, he was sticking two different needles of his own into his arm. Without hesitating Raymond shoved in a third needle, which was one of Jason's gifts, deep into his lower arm and stood up.

"Now who you think is the real man Mr. whatever your name is. I just wanted to show you dat drugs and children are my loves. You cain't play me. I know who you are. Here watch dis," he said while filling another needle and sticking it into his own neck. "Hummm," he said while losing his balance and stumbling into Jason's waiting arms.

"You might be right. Dis is some good shit. I still think mine's better. Here, you try some more," he said, while trying stick Jason with the same needle that he had just used.

Jason pushed him away and watched as Raymond crashed to the floor making enough noise to draw Raymond's woman out of the back room.

"Hey!" she said, "he's done overdost. How much did he take?" she asked.

"I think he should take a lot more," responded Jason with very serious look on his face.

"Get off of me woman I aint overdose'n. I'm just havin' fun with this pussy man whose real name is Oz. He thought I couldn't handle it, or that I didn't recognize his cute face," he said as he attempted to get up. Raymond was still talking but his voice was so slurred that they couldn't understand a word he was saying. His eyes were rolling and he was foaming at the mouth.

"You done shot yo-self-up," she said. "Well just lay back and rest," she told him.

"Where's mine?" she asked as she began to tie a piece of rubber around her upper arm. "I want some'a dat shit right now. He aint a-goin' nowhere wit out me," she hurriedly said.

Jason knew he had a choice to do what may be the right thing as the woman began to handle one of the needles. He could call an ambulance to save Raymond from his apparent overdose or he could get the two children and walk out of there and never look back. He chose the latter as he watched her anxiously inject herself with what was left in Raymond's needles.

He walked pass Raymond and his woman both now lying on the floor and he headed for the back room where the two children were locked in. He kicked in the door, picked up the little girl and grabbed the boy by the hand and lead them both out of the basement and out onto the street.

"Don't worry," he assured the two children, "you will both be all right as long as I have something to say about it."

# CHAPTER EIGHT

# Chester Bowls

*"And thou shalt not let any of thy seed pass through the fire to Molech, neither shalt thou profane the name of thy god: I am thy creator"*

(Leviticus 18:21)

### 4 WEEKS LATER

"Do you know a man named Chester Bowles", asked Helen.

"Actually, I'm not sure. He has been constantly in my latest dreams just like Victor and Raymond had been. Why, should I know such a man?" asked Jason in jest.

"I don't know, he sounded strangely familiar to me" said Helen. "There have been three messages on our home phone in the last two days. He just says, 'this is Chester Bowles, I want to talk to Oz', He said he got the number from the tow truck driver that towed his car from his accident at mile marker 99."

"Today when he called I answered the phone. He said he wanted to bring you a message. I told him to bring it by and that you would be here after 3 o'clock today. Of course, you weren't here and I was out in the parking lot talking to the lady in 2302 when he got off of the bus and he asked where you were by name. I kindly asked if I could help him and he walked directly up to me, looked me up and down and grinned showing a mouth filled with rotten teeth. I got a little uneasy but I thought if he knew you he must be friendly."

"Oh no, honey! I can't believe you would just accept someone's approach simply because they know my name. Babe you know better than that. What did he look like and what did he say?"

"He said to tell you that your friend Raymond had overdosed on drugs and he had left you a written note. He handed it to me and said to make sure you get it. When he had handed it to me he held on to it as I reached to get it. I tugged and he let it go while again grinning in a kind-of frightening way.

"Do you remember me?" he asked and answered his own question, "Naw, of course not. You thought yo nigga got rid of the likes of me long ago. But guess what, I'm still here work-n for yo daddy, the devil, and enjoying every minute of it. He knows I made it through. So… did you miss me, sweetie pie?" he asked, wearing a nasty grin.

"Uh? Do you Helen? Yeah you did… well after I take care of yo man I'll come give you one of your old Idle-wild Street treats," he said with a wink. He turned and walked back toward the bus stop while continuously looking over his shoulder.

"You're lucky, you're too old for me now," he said. 'I like'm young, but tell your man to stay away from me and my friends or I'll make an exception and make you mine again."

What he didn't know was someone had already done away with his two friends.

"Where is the note?" Jason asked with a very concerned look on his face.

Helen handed him the note and said, "I hate that evil man. And I don't even know him. There's something about him that stirs my inner fear as well as my wish to do him harm. If I didn't know better, I would believe that he is the same Chester that died at your hands while protecting little Sissy a long time ago. Maybe it's the name alone that turns my stomach," she said. "I think he is the devil's best friend"

"Yeah, well you're God's friend and there's no danger, but… caution is always warranted were evil lays its traps."

Jason read the note, Chester signed out by saying 'Thanks for another chance to make children sexually happy.' Jason stood up and quickly paced a few steps.

"That piece of shit has found his way back into another unsuspecting family with young children. Now he's taunting me with the prospect of what he intends to do to the babies. He's almost daring me to intervene. It sounds like a trap to draw me into his assigned plan to dispose of me and Oz forever. We'll see about that. I don't need help from my divine counterpart to handle a complete fool like him," said Jason.

"What do you plan on doing honey? That man is evil with his favorite friend being Satan himself. I'm worried that he will end up with the upper hand and prayer won't be enough to kill off the devil," Helen said.

"After all we've been through, you still don't seem to have enough faith in me or God,"

"What are you going to do? He knows where we live. We can't continue to go through life with a constant threat of being exploited by powers much stronger than us and more evil than we can even imagine. Please can we just pack up and move to another city. I have a cousin down in the Carolina's that have a small farm. Maybe we can go there and live happily ever-after, with nothing or no one seeking to take your life.

"Please, baby, let's just run and get out of the spiritual plight with this Chester and everyone else. Please…"

Jason hadn't heard a word she said. He was boiling inside and had no knowledge of what it meant to run from a child predator after so many years of running after them with Oz within.

"Game on…" he had instantly made up his mind that after Chester he would think of seeking peace through prayer and finding a hobby or learning to fish better as a sport. But right at this moment he had nothing on his mind but the thought of standing strong without Oz and challenging Chester and the evil that dwells inside of him and his devils. He could only think of putting on his amour and seeking a confrontation.

After more than a week of searching for the where a bouts of Chester, Jason began to conclude that like all true cowards Chester had gone into hiding. Until the phone rang in the middle of the night with the laughing voice he spoke. It was none other than Jason's most wanted enemy. Helen immediately handed the phone to Jason.

"I just wanted you to know that I'm aware that you are now responsible for the deaths of my pals Raymond and Victor. I don't know what to think of you, Mr. Jason. I was willing to let you and your old whore of a wife live, but now I can see you're much too stupid to mind your own business.

"I'm quite comfortable here with my new-found family and her 4 young ones that are eager to learn about the fun part of living, if you know what I mean. I also know that you have been looking for me. Shame on you trying to act like your Oz when I know for fact Oz has his hands full just explaining to your small-minded God as to why he can't learn to forgive and love the good loving men like me. Shame, shame, shame, these children here already have learned how pleasing I can be."

"Where are you, Chester? I've got a message for you in answer to the one you gave Helen," said Jason.

"Ah, yes, she is a cutie now that she's all grown up. Did she recognize me as her first lover from back when she turned four years old? I can't imagine how she could forget all those good nights me and her daddy shared with her while her mother pretended to be sleep. I miss her," he said sarcastically. "I wish I could do her one more time but she would be chasing me around and trying to rid herself from your boredom," said Chester while devilishly laughing.

"So… I ask again, where are you? Maybe I can help you find your god or tie you back to old oak tree where you spent so many good years, thanks to me and Oz," said Jason.

"You holier than thou bastard! I'll tell you where I am so I can rip your head off and feed your ass hole to the children that love me."

"That's no way to talk to your captor that caused you to suffer your own evil so gallantly. It wasn't Oz it was me just a plain old human being that took you and your friends to your captivity in chains," said Jason exaggerating the truth.

"You're a liar! I know it was Oz with his cruel out of control vengeance placed inside of you. You are nothing without his control over you. The others were afraid of him but I know he is wayward and he no longer has power over me. I need to rid the world of you before he can get back to your passage-way to physically being able to harm the servants of Moloch. In fact I am going to destroy you and impregnate your old ass wife to bare me a child so l can have a pure young lover like she was. Hah-hah-hah," Chester laughed and said. "I can't wait to watch you die at my hands." and hung up the phone.

"Son of a bitch," Jason said as he slammed down his own phone. "I want him so bad. I hope Oz doesn't get to him before I do as a man. I know he's nothing but a coward child molester that rapes and kills babies. I know that with God's help I can surely handle him alone. It would give me such pleasure to send him back to his maker destroyed by a mortal man he won't be able to live-on. It would disrupt their confidence that they are safe among us because we won't stand up and protect our own children. Please God just let me kill him with my own bare hands."

Helen just listened and showed signs of fear for her man. She knew he wasn't evil and without evil, killing is a bigger task than we can ever imagine.

She tearfully spoke "Please, honey, let's just leave here and let God and Oz bring him and his to their demise without us. Please, I know what a strong and brave man you are but we're just humans, those devils are possessed with evil spirits that only God can handle when he is ready."

"I am like Oz. I am God's tool. Who can stand against me with God by my side? I feel it, I know I won't be left to be defeated. Please Helen just have faith in me. I will win because God has made it so, I just don't know how it will happen but I know that it will."

A few more days went by. Chester knew that he had to act before Oz made his way back to Jason's human body to transition into flesh. He knew he had to strike while this man foolishly thought he had a chance to stand up to the power of evil without the power of an angel, even a wayward angel such as Oz. He needed to dispose of Jason now.

# CHAPTER NINE

# The Killing

"Mr. Jason my name is Ray-Ann, I'm 6 years old. I live on Kelly Street in the big white house across from the Zion Church. Please help me. Mr. Chester is hurting my little brother. He handed me his phone and told me to ask you, what you gonna do about it?" The child then quickly hung up.

Helen was on her way home but Jason had no intentions of waiting. He hurriedly grabbed his pistol and ran out the front door to drive the two-mile distance. Within minutes Jason pulled up in front of what he thought was the house in question. He quickly got out of his car and ran up the front porch steps and pounded on the door. Just then his phone rang.

"Where are you Mr. Jason it's me, your friend Chester. Come quickly I'm at your place with your woman sucking all over me... I'm very surprised you fell for that fake kid's call. I just wanted you out so me and your woman could spend a little time together before you get back here to let me take your life. By the way take your time getting back up here please, she's not quite done licking on me yet." With that Chester hung up the phone while laughing loud enough for Jason to boil over inside.

Fury has no patience. Jason was back and into his car tightly gripping his steering wheel and driving wildly up Bennett Street towards his home. The words coming from his mouth were a language so bad that he could not understand what he himself was saying.

Chester had made his way to Jason's home to complete his trap. He had waited for Helen to reach her door and insert the key, then he came up from behind her, grabbed her mouth and burst through the unlocked door with her before she knew what was happening. He knocked her to the floor with a hard punch to the face and proceeded to call Jason. Now he stood above Helen, looking down with his nasty grin, he kicked her and calmly said, "hi bitch". He partially closed the door and waiting for Jason to recklessly come running through it.

Low and behold within minutes Jason rushed in without thought or fear. Chester trip him as he came in just at the top of the foyer steps. Jason rolled down the stairs dropping his gun on the way. He quickly got back up to his feet only to be caught off guard with a hard, right-hand punch to the face. Chester picked up Jason's gun and smacked him across the head with it sending him into semi consciousness before Jason could even begin to fight back.

"Ha," he said, "I thought you were going to give me a little better fight than that. Look at ya now, lying on your back just like a dizzy tick on its back trying to stand up. If you were a woman or a child I'd stick you just for the intimidation," Chester said. Helen, also just as dizzy was trying to get to her feet to help Jason. Chester struck her again instantly sending her back to the floor.

"Now stay there until I get done with your man or boy, whatever he is to you." Chester walked back over to Jason and put Jason's own gun right up against his chest and fired a shot, "that was for Victor," he pulled the trigger again and said, "that was for Raymond," and then he fired once more, saying, "that one is for me and my god. I hope you and your Oz enjoy your journey to heaven's door. I'll take care of all your precious children and your woman when I get a chance."

Each shot had torn holes through Jason's clothes, right through his flesh and into his heart. As the blood began to pour out of Jason's chest Chester sat down the gun, lifted Jason up and dragged him over and sat him against the wall in a sitting position.

"Oh no you don't, you're not dying on me that easy, I want you to somehow bring Oz inside of you right now while suffering to the fact that his only passage into this human world is broken and defeated and to know that it's all over for you and him. No more playing the children's hero. I want you and him to be just plain old humanly and spiritually die right in front of your God's face while I masturbate as a celebration of Molect's victory."

Helen sneakily crawled and got her hands on the abandoned gun. She pointed it up at Chester while profusely shaking and pulled the trigger twice hitting him in the back and knocking him to the floor beside Jason. She then slowly got up to her feet and stood over the still smiling face of Chester and unloaded the pistil into is face and neck and clicked the gun several times after it was empty.

She slid down by Jason's side and held him while pleading with God, "Please, God, don't take him away. He is Your soldier… he is Your son… he is Your servant but… he's my love. Please don't take him from me. Take me instead or take me with him."

Simultaneously Oz was up in heaven and still undergoing the scrutiny of being judged by a host of angels. He was suddenly jolted by a striking pain in his heart as if someone had driven a hot sword into his chest again and again. His spirit form began to crumble likened to a thousand pieces of finely shattered diamonds.

"What is wrong my brother?" asked Chism with a look of fright and severe concern upon her spirited face. She quickly embraced and held him close to her heart, as if to become one with him.

"I don't know… it seems as if something is amiss with my spiritual connection to my human counterpart. I think Jason's life has been taken by evil," said Oz. "I have never felt this way before. I feel depleted and weak as if I too am losing the loving spirit that all life is made up of. I believe he is dying and I cannot I have no wish to be alive without him. Is this true Chism. Is my ability to be alive now connected to the mortal life of Jason?"

"Just hold on," said Chism. "This human to angelic connection has proven to be with the blessings of the Creator. We cannot assume that Satin can disrupt an assignment from the Father of all. Angels can't die unless at the hands of God and neither can the spirit of a human. The power of evil has gone too far. Go to Jason now and give him the strength of our God. I will not be far behind you."

"To the father I say, please send me. I do not wish to live on without his soul within me. Since God has joined us together our spirits should not be separable," said Oz.

"Then rise up and follow the instincts within you," said Chism to her comrade in this life's journey.

With those words Oz gathered himself and all the power within and he instantly found himself as Jason within the arms of Helen… dying without human hope.

Helen was still rocking Jason in her arms and pleading with him not to die. "Please, God, don't let death take his love from me. Please… he was just trying to do as you wanted. Don't let him die."

Oz was well within Jason now and fighting hard to not to give in to the acts of evil

Here on earth a neighbor hearing the shots fired called 911 and reported the incident. The police and ambulance arrived in a matter of minutes, guns drawn and prepared for the worst scenario. Helen was still lying right by Jason's side holding him tightly and still praying and crying when the medics entered. They quickly examined both Chester and Jason right there on the floor with Helen refusing to be pulled away from her man.

"They are both dead from gunshot wounds. Call the coroner's office there is nothing that we can do here for them," he said while attempting to lift Helen from the floor. "Miss, I'm sorry, his wounds are into his heart there's no way he can survive."

She just kept right on loudly crying, praying and holding him to her chest. Upon arrival at the hospital the emergency personnel pried Jason from Helen's arms. "I'm sorry miss we must get him inside to declare him DOA."

"No! He's not dead! Please do something. Honey, please tell them you're not dead. Please, look at him… he's moving, can't you see that he is moving?" Jason's body was completely still to the human eyes yet his facial expression wore the look of concern.

As they forcibly moved Helen away from Jason, another emergency room doctor entered and asked, "What have we got?"

Another answered, "Three gunshot wounds directly to his chest leaving a hole the size of a baseball through his back. Of course, he's not breathing, we have no heartbeat or pulse. Yet, he seems to be just waiting for something to be done to correct his problems."

Helen was now quietly standing nearby starry eyed, in a daze and covered with blood all over her clothing. She appeared very faint but still waiting for Jason to speak to her in a comforting way.

"Take him to A-11 and get the young lady into an intake room… and get her a sedative or something stronger. By the looks of her she's becoming silently hysterical and may go into complete shock at any moment if we don't do something fast."

As Jason lie momentarily motionless and alone in room A-11 with the spirit of Oz inside of his dead body, there was no thought, no vision of anything living and apparently no hope of surviving the gunshot wounds.

Helen willingly walked with the aid and was put under heavy sedation and placed in the room right next to Jason. An emergency room attendant was standing over Jason beginning to prep his body for the coroners' declaration of time of death. While looking into Jason's wound in amazement he paused and called out for someone to 'take a look at something very unusual.'

"Look at this," she said, "there is movement going on within his wound. It looks like his blood is glowing and moving with all kinds of different color sickle shaped particles that were growing and multiplying by the split seconds, "I've never seen anything like this before in my entire life. It looks like there are millions of microscopic cells building and repairing the damaged tissue right in front of my eyes"

"Move back a little and let me see," another demanded.

"I don't understand, did someone pour something onto him?"

"No, no one has been in here but me."

"You had better get someone from the lab to get in here right away, it may be something contagious."

Within minutes a lab technician entered into the room. By now the growth had covered all three entry bullet holes that had fractured Jason's rib cage, entered his heart and exited through his back. The wounds were still open but they appeared to now be ass a spider web of untorn flesh and bones. The bleeding had completely stopped and holes were filling with the same strange looking actively moving webs.

"Ummm, this is very strange. This instant growth appears to be some sort of fully alive illuminated sickle shaped cells," after a few seconds the technician simply said, "You know what… I don't believe he's dead."

"Don't be ridiculous; how could that be? He has no heart beat or pulse, what you mean you 'don't believe he's dead'. What else can he be if not dead?"

"I don't know, but his body is so warm that he feels like he has a fever. I've never felt a body that's supposedly dead this long and yet is still warmer than mine. I can't explain and I don't know for sure… but I still don't believe he is dead. His body seems to be healing itself as we speak. I think we need to get someone in here with a higher authority than yours or mine to decide how to proceed. In fact, I think someone of a much, much, higher authority is somehow already proceeding to work on this man's wounds."

"That's crazy, but hey… you're the boss. I'll call and get a specialist from the emergency operating staff to come down here now," he said while scurrying away.

# CHAPTER TEN

# Comatose

*Every abominable thing that the lord hates they have done for their gods*

(Deuteronomy 12:31)

*Both Jason and Oz were comatose for days. Helen wrote and read of GOD's birth according to her interpretation...*

A few weeks later with Jason still lying comatose and still undeclared as dead, Oz was unendingly praying and meditating about his own stubborn ways and now; with Jason dead in the hospital room at Mercy hospital. The miracles of life over death were in the healing process as both he and Jason were as one being watched over by Helen and Chism, and... seemingly protected from the sting of death by the Superior Creator.

After weeks of constant praying and crying each night for fear of losing her man Helen began to read to Jason as he lay motionless.

Day after day Helen read her own written novel (in the making) daily at Jason's bedside. She started each morning by speaking to him, "I love you" followed by the reading of her own written story lines.

"Jason… please hear me," she whispered. "Each day that I sit here by your side, I often hum while crying. I softly sing to let you know that I miss seeing your smiling eyes. I pray for the day of joy when I can listen to the beat of your precious heart next to mine. Or… I may hum quietly and sing under my breath to break the monotony of my constant prayer just to be able to hold you in my arms again.

"One set of acts reflect my own spiritual hunger to bring you back to us while the other reflects my praise for what you've meant to all those that love you… I wish, while setting here every day at your bedside, that I had said some of the things that I yearn to say now as your life has been put in jeopardy by an evil that you have chosen to stand against. I wish that I had told you between each word that I had spoken, that I love you.

"There is something about you that has embedded itself well inside of my soul. It is likened to the most beautiful visions for my eyes, food that satisfies the pains of a child's hunger. The smell of flowers that fill the air with pleasantry. And even my own rendition of the sound of a music that can calm the seas after a violent eternal storm.

"Music, music, music… it's the only thing that constantly whispers from my mind to your heart and soul as I pray to understand GOD. Somehow, she keeps the music playing and she leaves no path for death to follow.

"This, my love, is how my story of music and life begins, starting from the beginning of time up until now… I write about God as she may have brought all things into existence. I know you may find it all far-fetched nowadays that music has become the goddess driven path to prayer and celebration of life. Without you here with me my strong imagination allows me to venture into what may have been.

"I can't write about life's romances or loving families or exciting Hollywood type adventures, so I have written about my dreams of what could have been just as well as what we have excepted as biblical truths. In light of all that has happened to us over the years I decided to write about our creator.

"Though we know nothing of what truly occurred thousands of years ago and before mankind, it saves my sole to paint a place that was built upon the beauty of sound," Helen said while holding his hand within one of hers and positioning herself to be able to turn her own written pages while reading to him.

"So… if you can hear me honey, I hope it's as pleasant for you to listen to as it has been for me to write and now read to you each day. It's going to help me stay sane while knowing God won't take you from me or I won't be able to finish writing Her life's story," Helen said with a slight smile on her face as if God might care or as if Jason could actually hear her.

"And if you are listening please don't laugh because even this; what some might say 'is a farfetched story', could truly be the way it is and what may have all happened.

"In this beginning… just six days before the birth of man. There was no motion, light, nor sound. There was absolutely no sign of life as life has been known to us throughout our existence. All was still and motionless. For thousands of years every void, if there was such thing as voids, had been filled with nothingness.

"And then… from somewhere out in that dark stillness came a soft sweet humming sound. The humming was joined by what resembles the random quiet whispering of wind chimes and bells. At first… very mysterious and ever so slight… then, a little louder as the motions of the universe seemed to be intentionally awakened by an unknown force. The sound, on its own, slowly became organized, beautiful and fulfilling to all of the creative spirits as it carried into to the darkness throughout all existing spaces…

"It carried on for what seemed to have lasted a million years when suddenly and without warning the calmness and musical peace was disrupted by a totally silent explosion of dancing motions of light from every direction. There was a sparkling array of brightness and colors that reached just past the edge of all existence, surprising even… God… Herself.

"And then… the showers of light simmered down falling everywhere likened to the dying sparks of one of today's firework displays. The gentle sound of Her humming returned to center stage. She continued to softly hum with the harmony of the wind chimes and now the many other known and unknown natural sounds that could be heard in Her musical background.

"On some moonlit nights, if you listen closely, you can hear Her as I can even hear Her here and now... You must listen closely for Her music that is buried well within your own inner mind. It can always be heard; every minute, every hour of every day.'

Are you listening to me with an open mind my love? Please hear my story of God's love, for this in itself is a very special moment. I hope you are listening and making your way back to life just as God's sounds of music gave life to the universe. It was soft and tender and all within the first life-giving breath of the mother of God. It was followed by a forever glorious sound that will always exist.

"The man, God Himself, was being lovingly born and spiritually mesmerized by Her songs of love and compassion. All of this was accelerated through a time that was, is and will be. She kissed the forehead of Her new born son while planting a certain spiritual rhythm into His soul. All of Her creative motions were turned into those soft and loving sounds that were instilled in Him with all there was to ever know. This was the seventh day of creation... His magnificent beginning.

"So... music began on the day our man God was born. And the song was His name and will always remain deeply embedded in the hearts, minds and the spirits of all that are brought to life.

"In these days the trees in the forest often danced to the musical sounds of the winds as they blow where there are no human ears to listen or to see them dancing.

"The oceans perform with the forever sustaining rhythm of the gravitational force along the thousands of miles of the lovely shorelines of our seas.

"Thunder often rolls out its deep sounding bass that can shake the very earth that we walk upon with a sudden flash and crack of lightning to start or mark the end of its concert.

"Even a slight breeze of the wind carries itself to the chasms of our inner minds with the same whispering sound that fills a hand cuffed sea shell held to our ears.

"And ah, my sleeping Jason, don't forget the sweet pitter-pattering sound of a summer rain as it cools the sun heated sidewalks of today. As a writer I could go on and on with all the many musical sounds that we hear and yet take for granted as being coincidental acts and noises of nature. A blessing is to be able to distinguish the heart felt messages built within the sounds that surround all of Her creations.

"Life was music and Her music was His song now and for all of life's pleasures still to come. Without knowing the song, we cannot know His name; for the melody and lyrics of Her song to Him and His name are one of the same. The song is just as long as the seventh day. And He shall remain Her song as well as Her child eternally.

"On that day the sounds of creation, the sounds of celebration and joy, filled the darkness far beyond this part of heaven and earth that had been created just for us even beyond Him.

"As time passed came the evolved sounds of these two creative souls became separated by acts of destiny. They began to part... As She moved away from the God child, He painfully cried and desperately reached out to Her. The music of His longing and desire was as sweet as any sound could ever be, but… what can possibly be sweeter or more moving than the sounds that a child makes while reaching for his or her mother's love in desperation while being parted?

"Like the lyrics of unending love songs, His spiritual love for Her presence and Her voice went on. With that certain melody She had placed within Him, the knowledge of all things and of life everlasting. She had set His path before Him without doubt. The newly born creator was and will be the pulse of what is good and challenging for all of mankind to come. She was pleased and went off to Her place of rest…

"So… the first sound of music was truly the humming of the Creator. In time, the splendor of harmony was performed by Her own host of creations.

*"'Jubal, the father of all those who played the harp and the flute'*

(Genesis: 4:21)

"They knew that all sounds could be music or… just simply noises that could ultimately be heard by the spirits of all living things of nature. Music can be pleasing, noise can be suffering just as acts of good and bad. And so… it may be written that the creations of God began to look upon and teach the descendants of human creation long before the era of Adam began.

"To this day when an infant smiles he or she is responding to the heavenly gentle healing sound of God's loving voice. It is music. When we grow away from Her voice we begin to cry in fear of being lost to our own lust of becoming as loving as She.

"When we grow on, we learn to rely upon each other's instinct to compete for the loving sounds heard only through the ears of mankind. Without Her spiritual voice and lessons of perfection, we begin to go through the growing pains of things that will naturally occur. The songs within us of the spirit will never end but songs directed to the ears of men will fade just as motions of the sea cease and move into stillness. Without movement sounds and noises of men can only exist within our spiritual existence.

"Many thousands of years have passed as the sounds of communication with God have become sounds that are heard only through the ears of men and beast instead of their spiritual minds and souls. The gifted ability of infants to hear the voice of God are partially taken away upon the age of reasoning. The disabling wishes of choice have been mastered by most of mankind and now they too hear the self-guided noises of his earthly brothers.

"The sounds we hear and believe in have become avenues of fate. The voices of flesh and blood have become a choir of nature that is needed in order to live within our physical boundaries set by the imperfections of natural phenomena.

"As mankind we have learned to disobey our spiritual instructions and have forgotten the formula of our own music of the soul. Our music begins to lack the pleasures of God's love and tranquility. We mistakenly have learned to yearn for the driving sounds of self-passion and the pleasures of danger and jealousy.

"We began to submit to the power of unconquerable obstacles that stand between us and God. Without the sound of Her voice we convince ourselves that Her majestic perfections can be achieved through our own dominance and self-praise. We've learned to control the minds of others through our own ability to create a spiritual lust by intoxicating sound itself with body movements, beauty to the eyes and the proud arrogant faces of mankind.

"We send the subliminal message that says, craving this human-made feeling of what we claim is of God, is the purpose of life and the ultimate reward of being alive. It becomes an acclaimed part of our reproduction and our growing from individuals into being the many of ourselves."

***

Suddenly in a groggy whisper and with a slight smile Jason spoke out,

"How on earth did you come up with a story like that?"

"Oh my God honey your awoke!" Exclaimed Helen while spontaneously dropping her book to bend down and squeeze him tightly against her. "Thank you, God! Thank you, God! Oh, thank you, God! Baby I'm so glad to have you back here with me. Please tell me you are all right.

*"Doctor! Nurse! Somebody help me! He's awake!*

"I knew God wouldn't let you die, I knew it!"

She got up and ran to the nurse's station. "Please hurry, my man is awake and has spoken to me. Please, come quickly!"

As the nurses scrambled, they summoned the doctor and the STAT team for the anticipated emergency. When they got into Jason's room, he lay there unchanged but smiling from ear to ear as if to wonder what all the commotion was about.

But, there had been no change in his condition. He was still dead according to his vital monitors. The disappointment filled the room as they all began to sadly exit. Helen was franticly tapping on all of the monitoring equipment within her reach.

"Wait! Don't leave. This shit aint workin'. My man spoke to me just a moment ago. Please! I'm not crazy. He talked to me. Please check him, don't' just look at the monitor screens.

And then… suddenly, to their dismay one of the team seen Jason slightly move his hand and he smiled even more. The astonish staff quickly turned around and re-entered the room to examine him in every way. His pulse, his blood pressure, everything they checked was strangely now reading strong and normal. Jason had miraculously recovered both up on the screens above and their hands-on procedures.

After a short examination, the astonished STAT team left Helen alone with her miracle man. Both Jason and Helen were speechless. Finally, after sitting and touching each other for what seemed like forever, Jason managed to speak again, "You still haven't told me where you got the notion that your Creator was the mother of our God. That story of music being introduced by a female God thousands of years ago and how she loved her Son and how her Son and music connected forever through her sounds of love.

"You didn't think I was listening, did you?" Jason asked with wearing the loving grin he wore just for Helen.

"I got it from my own recent dreams and nightmares while sitting here by your side day after day and night after night praying that you would come back to me. Why? Do you think it's not possible that a She instead of a He could bring both powers into being?" Helen replied.

"No, I mean yes, I do believe it could be but it is a little scary to think all those things may have actually happened and you made it sound as if it was just a short moment ago. I found myself wanting to listen for the sound of the whispering chimes, just to see if I could hear and feel the comfort of God's music the way it was meant to be.

"And wow, to suggest that God is a female may be too much to comprehend. In addition to the gender issue, were you trying to say that sound came to life because it's a result of a motion or that motion is the only way that sound can be made. Or… that they are one of the same?

"Or… wait, let me try it this way, if something cannot move at all it cannot make a sound? I was attempting to move and let you know that I was alive and thinking and feeling love and listening for the sweet music you were describing. For a moment there I even attempted to dance a little in my efforts in letting you know that I was listening."

"Do you want to talk about this or would you rather talk about what happen that night with Chester trying to hurt you?" asked Helen.

"Please I don't want to talk about any Chester or anyone in that world of craziness for at least the next thousand years, but where is he now? Did Oz get to him? Did he harm you honey? I'm so sorry I didn't protect you from that snake. During my unconsciousness, I dreamt of him and his evil god, smiling every moment. At times I even had him by his throat choking him. But every time I killed him dead he stood up and took on another body from hell." Jason said.

"Please honey we don't have talk about him or them now or ever. Let's just let God handle all those that She hates so much." Helen said, while again pulling Jason closer to her chest. "I was crying just for you while trying to pray as I kept feeling Her presence here while you were fighting for your life, that organized sound of sacred music in itself was my salvation. It can become a god that is in possession of one of the many powers of our Creator.

"Music can heal and mold complete cultures into worship like states of minds that are capable of being strong enough to match the power of prayer when it's not being manipulated by deceptive gods that are created by mankind. Angelic gods, for whatever the reason, may thrive on the power of what we call evil and condescending acts.

"God, Her son, often speaks in His written biblical word of an evil that lurks in the hearts and minds of His own angelic creations. I am saying that if one controls the love of music he can also controls the level of worship that may be stolen from an unknowing soul," Helen remarked.

She continued, "While we are speaking of stories of old, listen to my rendition of a dream I had just two nights ago while sitting here at your bedside I believed it was generated by my constant prayers for you and by all those stories you use to tell me of the many so-called writings of 'missing' or 'lost books' of the bible. It went something like this:"

"No wait, honey! You haven't told me where he is or what happened to him. Did Oz kill him? Please tell me he did."

Helen began to sob. "Okay, okay. No, no one killed him but me. I shot him a thousand times with your gun. And I hope God took him to hell," she said while continuing to sob.

"While he was here dead, someone broke into the morgue and stole his body. I hope whoever did it continued to kill everything that he stood for. I killed him for you, honey. He was rot and he tried to take you away from me, but God wouldn't let him.

"Please, honey, let's just talk about my dreams of music and our female God. Please, honey, please. You see, I dreamed I was flying in what seemed to be a helicopter at a very high rate of speed just inches above the tree tops of a super huge jungle area. There was no source of light on the ground anywhere, just the quick moving silhouettes of the thousands of tree tops that were brightly lit by the moon and star light.

"It seemed like we were flying low enough for the helicopter blades to brush against the tree tops of the tallest trees in the valleys. Just before I woke we had flown over an area that was lit up by many scattered blazing camp fires with hundreds of people dancing around them with all faces looking up to the skies above.

"And do you know what was strange? The music that I think I heard wasn't the drum beat that you would think should be coming from what seemed to be a prehistoric jungle. It sounded loud and booming like the noise we hear these days by cars being driven around in the middle of the night right here in the middle of East Hills," said Helen.

Jason interrupted; "Boy, do I know that nauseating sleep interrupting sound. It drives me crazy. Why do you think they need to play it loud enough to shake our windowpanes? Sometimes, the base noise vibrates my stomach and makes me suddenly feel sick inside. What makes them think they should be able to intrude into the peaceful privacy of others without care or respect? Sometimes I felt like going outside and yanking one of them out of their cars along with the huge speakers they've placed inside the trunks of the car, the bumpers, or wherever else they may be.

"I'm often amazed that as we are a race of people that often can't afford to listen to free music and yet they spend tremendous amounts of money in an attempt to entertain people at large with their choice of what I call plain ole untalented noise to dance too. Somehow, it stirs me to a point of frustration and even a momentary dislike of music, period. I've seen men well into the age of their fifties blasting their beat as if they are the ones actually playing the bass instrument. They bobble and jerk their heads while making strange faces, as if they are on a stage trying to cause someone to look and approve of them being the center attraction as they drive down the avenue out of ear range.

"It's usually not long before the next wannabe entertainer comes along as if it's his turn to be the star of the show, and to show that his speakers are louder. Ironically, they all seem to be playing the same-ole vibrating beat. I often wonder if there is anyone that actually likes those side shows that drive through the neighborhood or are they like us, wondering why in the hell would anyone do it to entertain people outside of their own car.

"It's imposing and shows how goofy we can be once given an imaginary stage of our own," said Jason. "Anyway, back to your dream story."

"One by one the sons of God yielded to the rhythm of temptation and to their own desires to be self-indulgent. God had failed. The gift of choice had been placed deeply into the free minds of the inhabitants of heaven, and earth. The ability to stay connected to our Creator and His or Her ways were slowly being discarded.

"The idea of giving choices to mankind can be much like the toss of a coin, add the attraction of sight and sound coupled with the disconnect of spiritual guidance and we find ourselves yielding not only to temptation but to all hope of finding our purpose for life beyond living for self-worship and acclaim. This disconnect seems to lead us to what is a lifelong moment of folly rather than the desire of love, peace, respect and tranquility.

"Anyway.... the daughters of men below were dancing hard and violent in a competitive way; pushing and shoving each other aside so they could be perhaps seen and chosen by the spectators from above. I've often thought it must have been this way to win the attention of the seraphim or angelic sons of God so they could become mothers for those they thought would take them into heaven's better place.

"According to the bible, 'one by one the sons of God left the bosoms of the Creator. One by one they yielded and sexually indulged with the daughters of men which were the earthly women of the night.'

"Like the arenas and stadiums of today the view from the perches of the high places where the sons of God dwelt provided a balcony-like observation point. Nightly they could enjoy the show of shows; the magical sounds of music and the provocative dancing performed throughout the night by the spellbind daughters of men.

"What could not be seen by their lustfully hungry eyes was the desires that were easily stirring in the hearts of the supposedly honorable minds of the holy angels that were being driven by lust and love at the thought of the god like power to master a soul and even reproduce themselves, as God had said 'be fruitful and multiply'.

"They had given in to the thought of human nature instead of God's disciplined. It all directly equated to an inability to comprehend or to foresee the consequences of acts of disobedience that could lead to self-destruction. The rules of God became clouded by the desires of the sons of God that had yearned for the daughters of men for the rewards of passion.

"So... a modern way to put it, I guess that many of them came down from the heavens and 'got a little bit' under the midnight moon and the enticement of the soul stirring music and dancing," Helen said.

"Are you sure you want to hear about my silly hospital bedside dreams?" she blushed and smiled at him as if she wasn't aware of the powers that women have over the natural lustfulness instilled in most males for the purpose of reproduction.

"In order to dance with such powerful spiritual and sexual attractiveness they must have had the magical intoxication of what music can be made of. Their bodies seemed to involuntarily respond to each and every beat. The instrument used couldn't have mattered, it could have been the beat of percussion, the strings of a harp, the clapping of hands, the stomping of feet, a hum, a whistle or just singing voices. All likes of organized sound that can set our bodies into seductive motion.

"The stage was set... On those warm summer nights near what may have been the biblical site of the Garden of Eden, the music of the night was played at its best. The daughters of men danced to the beat as if they instinctively understood the temptation that had been placed into the hearts of those above.

"They had come to know the natural yearnings for intimate contact with the huge angel-like, well-proportioned God gifted sons of God. Angels were thought to be pure at heart and sacredly protected by the Creator of all things.

"Down in the valley of the daughters of men they were dressed in their night attire. It was scant and tempting to the eyes of any and all that gazed upon them. They were shapely and wore facial expressions that were nothing short of luscious, somewhat like the icons of today's world.

"Their skin appeared like light brown velvet under the light of the moon and stars. Their lips were made moist with red colored oils and the eyes behind the extended lashes along with the dance motion of their shapely bodies could penetrate well into whatever caused the angel-like males from above to understandably lose self-control.

"Their wishes were to entice those above to touch and excite themselves in some way to cause total submission to the point of being willing to sacrifice their body and souls and keep them as their own possessions. On the ground below, they were willing to pay any price for the prize of intercourse and their own ultimate satisfaction that not even a god could resist.

"The lust became stronger than the will to live. The angels had no choice but to yield. They, unknowingly, were ready to give their lives for a chance of becoming immortal through the pleasurable act that would lead to the God forbidden reproduction between the two different creations. And the beat went on, realistically the reward of sexual pleasures has no match known to man," said Helen.

"Does this mean that music played a part in these acts of disobedience or is it just a part of the web like trap of temptation for both gods and humans of both genders? The answer could certainly be 'yes,'" said Jason, answering his own question.

Helen went on to say, "I think that in the thousands of years gone by and also currently, people of African descent have been extremely susceptible to all music. Organized, unorganized, readable and unreadable music that can be blindly felt spiritually. Musical notes, musical translations and the mystical instructions coming to us subliminally are typically heard only through human ears by all other races.

"Our devotion and innocence towards others and their sounds have made us and some other music driven people, privileged to feel the meaning of the musical messages and directions from what was believed to be a higher spiritual realm. Music has kept us in touch with our own inner souls. We danced to a different beat than that which controls the masses of the world.

"Unfortunately, these days we seem to dance to any and every beat taken in by our ears. To many people this seems to have taken us into many frivolous directions that could be controlled by the evils of our own over indulgence and misconceptions.

"Many of us are hopeful in thinking that the DNA in our blood, no matter what beat we dance to, will lead us to the brink of salvation and back to the understanding of the wishes of our Creator when it comes to soul felt sounds that could very well enable us to sustain happiness and protection under the spirits of what may be called 'good,'" speculated Helen.

"You know, Helen, not so long ago, I thought you loved music just like the rest of us," said Jason.

"I thought I did to. I'm not as sure any more based on these dreams while praying so hard for you, I'm beginning to think it has a way of controlling our sense of reality. It seems to be able to make us vulnerable to bad choices as if we can't hear above the noise while our souls are being stolen. It can lift us up and take us down while evil laughs to the same beat. It has been the special rise and fall of many of our celebrities in recent times.

"Remember Michael, Whitney, Ruffin, Holiday and many more. They all may have been snared by what could have been the evil's 'let's make a deal' scenario to greatness. Who knows, maybe the mesmerizing sounds opens too many doors with-in our minds."

"Now that is scary," said Jason, "but why are you trying to blame music for the mistakes that people seem to make while under the influence of drugs. Everyone doesn't go off the edge. Most people are just trying to enjoy their own God gifted talents and the good feelings we get while dancing in a fun way to take off the stress and stuffiness and: are just trying to figure out what to do to bring us together in celebration of one thing or another.

"I, for one, enjoy dancing with the thought that everyone is looking at just me while I personally entertain the world of onlookers with my little steps that give me the feeling of being a special dancer that can bring a special joy to the party. How could anything bad come from something that brings such a good feeling of a little stardom into our lives?" he questioned.

"I know that our intentions aren't always to go beyond the boundaries of what is called fun and lightheartedness but it could be that we become vulnerable to the same feeling that came over women that danced and sang for sexual enticement of God's angels without realizing what the suggestive movements are generating in the inner minds of the opposite sex or these days, even the same sex," said Helen

She tilted her head and stood closer while looking her mate directly in the face. "So, which one is it, the music or the body motions that we respond with that may result in criminal activity?

"I love music. Sometimes when I'm alone, it does something to my mind that nothing else can. It brings back memories. It causes me to feel loved. It bridges sadness to happiness. Sometimes, I even view things in my mind that seem to coincide with the music that's playing. What would a movie be without music building up the expectations of what is about happen, or… the mellow mood of a scene that introduces passion to a romantic setting?

"Even todays rap music, in its place, often causes me to tap my feet and bounce my head to its beat. It has surely become a crowd pleaser when comes to the liveliness needed to get everyone dancing to the same beat.

"I don't know sweetheart… It's going to take a lot to convince anyone these days that music may have a negative effect on anything under the sun, except maybe being stir crazy from the effects of an empty or soundless mind."

"Well, you may be right about all that you have said. But I must still say that I'm very suspicious of some of today's fallout from music written around violence and gender insults. Sometimes, it seems as if they attempt to give out a dumb gangster image rather than one of artistic talent or… even a touch of a meaningful message would be nice.

"I realize that different age groups of people like and dislike the music's that are popular within their own times based mainly upon old fashion reasoning. I'm personally more concerned about those of us that make music an imperative part of our moment to moment lives until we are consumed and obsessed with filling every second with idleness and one sound or another, there is no men-tal quietness or serenity left to enjoy," responded Jason.

"Well, Jason," Helen came back with the same as-a-matter-of-fact-snobiness as Jason, "I'm a grown woman… a woman that has had my share of ups and downs with happiness and a lot of self-made heart break-ing moments. There have been times in my past that I've been a little sinful bitch as a brown woman from Home-wood, Pennsylvania.

"There have been many times that I've consciously made bad decisions with my eyes wide open. When it comes to music, I can recall shaking my tail feathers with the best of them. With my skirt pulled well above my knees to show my legs and a little bit of my lower thighs while wearing my deviously sexy dance face for all of the male on-looking eyes.

"There have been times that I've made sure that my breast line was a little more in sight than usual and slightly oiled to bring out their smoothness and my color of brown. I've enjoyed a chilled glass of wine with soft music in the background as my trap for a man while making myself feel even more promiscuous with false eye lashes, smelly perfumes and revealing under-cloths.

"All these types of things I consider girly sins that get us into trouble within the human brains of the average female. But… and this is a big size but, I'm not evil. I haven't plotted a death or gone out at night to rob old ladies or to harm other people with nasty gossip and I haven't even shop lifted lately," she said with a childish smile.

"I've said all this because I would like you and everyone that ever reads my up-coming book about music to know that despite the downfalls of drugs and alcohol, music has much more to give than it has ever taken. And that, despite my many mistakes and misjudgments about the good and bad things, including the music in our lives, guess what…? God still loves me.

"So, please be careful of how you attack the devil while he is so interwoven in the fabric of music itself. And oh… by the way, I was wrong when I said I love music, I should have said I don't know how I would live without it, especial since I've written so much about it in my book to you that God herself brought it to life, along with Her first born son…," she said, as she dipped her head a little while making selfie-styled mirror puckered lips and suddenly shut-up talking.

"Hey!" Jason said in a slightly joking manner, "you are *not* supposed to correct your man like that. Yours is my book, I can be wrong if I want to," he said while teasingly smiling at her.

THE POEM

# Pray for Our God

When the Spirit of music leads us away from what is good it in itself has become the unworthy god of worship and self-destruction.

For those of us that are unorganized noise makers: I personally believe it all may have started with the bible quote 'Make a joyful noise unto the lord.'

That simple statement could lead to the un-emotional noise and the singing of praises to those that are just kings or a certain kind of self-proclaimed man who suffers with the decease of his own beat to self-recognition. In my own heart I know that even God did not compose songs about Him or Herself. He or She, listens to the cries, heart beats and rhythms of heartfelt contentment within their own creations. Then and only then can they be loved and protected from themselves or supernatural extinction.

Again, I say… every sound can be construed as music. Every movement can be construed as a dance. Often, we walk slowly to our own beat that only we can hear. We can speed up our breathing, and the beat in our minds immediately adjust. We can think up the sound of voices or the noise of any instrument and we clearly hear the music that we just heard a moment ago even after the song has ended. A favorite song that may have been hummed to us years ago sticks in our minds. We can hear someone whistle a tune and create the song in our thoughts and repeat it silently hour after hour unable to end the song that we may not even know the words too. There are times when someone walks by and embeds a melody into our minds and we can still hear it even though they are gone by and long out of reach of hearing the passer-by. There are times we can't shake a sound that we have just heard until another song sets itself in our mind and then with-in minutes we can't re-call the previous beat that we were obsessed with a moment ago.

Some folk can instantly like music that they had never heard before or instantly become annoyed by sounds that they may later find themselves in love with. Music can easily remind us of a special time in our life or remind us of a person or place that has long been forgotten.

There are times when we remember lyrics to a song that we have forgotten until we hear it being sung, whistled or hummed by or another… and then we can easily sing along, often surprising ourselves with an un-intended recall of not only the words but the unmistakable beat.

Most of us find ourselves patting our feet, snapping our fingers or moving our shoulders from side to side even when we have never heard the song. As a black man with love for the music of his times (in my case '60s and '70s) I can personally recognize thousands of tunes after a few beats of a song played. I always astonish myself at the ability to know what words and the beats are ahead.

I once attended a Michael Jackson concert where a few beats of his song were played and the crowd was on their feet screaming with an instant recognition of the song that was about to be sung.

What's even more astonishing is when we can instantly recognize a missed beat, or wrong words, at times identifying that it is the wrong voice or entertainer without a doubt.

Humans are exclusive to the making of music with changes of sounds and beats. Birds do sing. Bees seem to hum. Most animals learn to make mating calls. Crickets chirp throughout the night. Frogs add a special tone by their rib-bit noises. Some owls seem to always ask for identification with the repeated question of whoo-whoo-whoooooo.

A lion and a lot of felines can shake the ground with a roar that most brave men fear or… they can calm the jungle with a purr. The timber wolf can howl by the light of the silvery moon. Even the dolphins and many other sea creatures can make sounds that untalented humans often seem to attempt to mimic when we are in pain; but even when we are in pain we moan with a rhythm or give out a fading scream.

To some of us, country western singers seem to attempt to sing without moving their lips. Rappers attempt to hear their dancing and motions without a stand out voice. Opera singers seem to have pure voice control with unidentifiable words and a well-orchestrated sound of instruments.

Soul singers have mastered the expression of love and pain with voices of harmony as their musical background setting and beat. There doesn't seem to be any instrument that they cannot emulate with voices. They can easily set a visual with group dance steps based upon rhythmic stomps and hand claps.

Choirs belt out enough volume to be heard from the mountainside and often into the heavens above; sometimes moving side to side but careful not to over dance for fear of losing the congregational spirit.

Hard rockers seem to be sold on creating as much sound as they can, often without a melody or rhythm that some of us can even begin to understand.

Crooners can make many of us fall in love with the smooth moves, eye movement and lyrics that cause the word love to be the starting point of child birth…

Music has often been used to lead men into battles even in the presence of God, or; especially in the presence of God. Liken to drugs and alcohol, music has been used as a tool to enhance rituals and celebrations to a point of uncontrollable vulnerability to unacceptable acts that have been known to control cultures in different centuries all over the world. I don't think it can inspire hate… thank God for that… Or can it?" she asked while tenderly squeezing Jason's hand.

"I truly don't know," Jason sadly answered at a whispering tone of voice. "What I just went through as a result of what does exist at mile marker 99, leads me to believe that the heavenly world has so many aspects of life that we as humans can't even begin to imagine what should or shouldn't be.

Even if we do attempt to understand and encounter that could possibly be a connection between evil having access to our minds and spirits through the presentation of music or anything else that can influence our thoughtless and self-serving actions, we will always fall short of understanding why.

Subliminal evil powers can direct us into serving a god of its own choice, your choice, or the choice of gods that can orchestrate the worst and the most uncontrollable evil acts that humans can imagine.

I, for one, at this moment, am not sure if I am alive or dead, yet I seem to be experiencing a moment of wisdom far beyond my own ability. All that I think I know is that I want to do my best to do the right thing based upon the instinct of human and spiritual love and compassion.

God's wishes, whether the creator is female, (as in your story) or male, (like we've always been taught), may be very well predicated upon the daily actions that we are instilled to take part in that satisfies the very compassions that we are born to fulfill just for the sake of completing a single verse of His or Her song that leads to the perfection of all that is…

Personally, at this moment, I kind-of believe that we all have a task, and that task is to live with-in a positive light, sound and wellbeing that will enable us all to understand why some things must temporarily die off while others predictably move into the perfection of God's final concert of complete harmony.

And then… and only then… the song comes to an end but never ceases to play when its needed to lift the spirits of God's children.

Again, I say… its kind-of like; the breast that feeds us all has finally been found, the hunger ceases and the bliss of satisfaction has been provided to all that have learned to love. I guess for obvious human reasons, being female gets my vote if it comes to God's gender… (A smile from Jason, a thumbs up from Helen)


In Jason's mind was the song by Johnny Nash, "I Can See Clearly Now the Rain has Gone."

# The End

# About the humble author: Jack Thomas Reynolds

A dedicated friend, and brother, and… father of six that dreams of being their hero, not as a super person, but more as a watchful mind that has learned just enough to contribute just a taste of happiness along with an answered special prayer that may assure safety and love when they need it most.